Jane's favorite retreat was Manhattan's Battery Park. When her mother departed without a crumb of warning for an ashram in India, Jane extended her search for solace to the Staten Island ferry. On an impulse she took the train to Tottenville, the end of the line. There she discovered a mysterious bar with a juke box that played only songs from World War II and a strange fascinating young man who introduced her to cognac and Sinatra instead of grass and rock. Filled with nostalgia for a time she had never known, Jane vacillated between the reality of the attractive, astrology-minded "Scorpio" and the unreality of a homelife in total chaos.

HOPE CAMPBELL confesses that *No More Trains to Tottenville* was born of wishful thinking. Unable to go to India, she went to Staten Island instead; and while riding the Tottenville train she began to wonder what young people might learn, not only from their parents' sudden absence but from a taste of the time of their parents' youth.

THE LAUREL-LEAF LIBRARY brings together under a single imprint outstanding works of fiction and nonfiction particularly suitable for young adult readers, both in and out of the classroom. This series is under the editorship of M. Jerry Weiss, Distinguished Professor of Communications, Jersey City State College, and Charles F. Reasoner, Professor of Elementary Education, New York University.

No More Trains to Tottenville

HOPE CAMPBELL

TO RENEE AND JANE AND HEIDI

Published by
Dell Publishing Co., Inc.
750 Third Avenue
New York, New York 10017

Laurel-Leaf Library ® TM 766734, Dell Publishing Co., Inc.
Reprinted by arrangement with McCall Books,
a division of Saturday Review Press.
Printed in the United States of America
First Laurel printing—September 1972

One

"I'm sorry but I've had it!" said my mother with a wild look at my father.

She often prefixes such modern statements with just such an old-fashioned apology because she was so well brought up and is basically so polite. But one shouldn't pay any attention to these good-mannered beginnings. The things to listen for are at the end of her sentences, such as, "I've had it!"

She whirled on me with a pointed finger that looked very sure of itself. "I'm sick and tired of this entire runaway generation. If you think there's a generation gap *now*, just wait. As far as I'm concerned it isn't nearly wide enough. I'm ready to make a real hole in it. From here to Tibet!"

The finger jabbed very forcefully through the air in my direction. "If I hear one more word about running away—one *peep*—the one who's going to do the running is *me*. I mean it. I'm sorry but I've had it!" she repeated unnecessarily.

Well, I knew she'd had it, but of course she wasn't going to run away. That was the most ridiculous thing I'd ever heard!

We were in our living room, it was very late at night, and mother was still in her blue suit skirt, a rumpled white blouse, with her brown hair messed on one side and neat on the other. She hadn't undressed to go to bed and she had terrible circles under her eyes. Mother is about my size, and has a nice, thin-featured, longish sort of face. Now that she's getting older she's put on a little weight but not much. She still looks young except for those circles which she's had all her life and which always get worse when she's tired.

I should have felt guilty but I didn't, even though I knew what was the matter. She was worn out, exhausted. Mother had a very demanding job in a public relations firm, and beyond that there was my father, my brother, and me. Right now she'd "had it" with all of us.

In that statement she was including my older brother, Dick, who was supposed to be in prep school but wasn't because he'd split to sit in on a college demonstration in another state and then decided to stay indefinitely and not go back. It was a very liberal, non-accredited college that didn't care about these things, so he was living around the dorms, smoking lots of grass, and what not. My mother had called the college several times, but the permissive faculty could never seem to locate him or any of his friends.

Since she had been working for many years to supplement the income so we could both go to private schools, as she and my father had, she was a little irritated. Prep school was a crucial step toward Dick's college education. Also, mother had paid the tuition for the entire year. She always did that so the money couldn't be tapped for anything else. And Dick hadn't been at school for the past two and a half months. In spite of that, we'd hear from him occasionally when he wanted money for food. That's what he said, of course. I knew what he *really* wanted money for, and so did my mother. But my father chose to ignore the grass scene, and once, acting a bit like the faculty, even sent him five whole dollars! Ostensibly for a case of canned beans.

That was another thing. My father refused to go up there, find Dick, remove him, and drag him back, bodily if necessary, to his own school. Instead he complained bitterly that mother never should have paid the tuition in advance! In that way he implied that she was to blame for the whole thing, and it made her *furious.* He proclaimed that Richard, at eighteen, was old enough to be on his own, that he would have to lead his own life and make his own mistakes. If he was stupid enough to pull this stunt, the consequences were on his head! My father refused to have anything to do with it. He certainly had a point, but she had a point, too. She insisted that Dick must at least finish his senior year, and since she had worked so hard to get him a really fine education, he had a moral obligation to do so. They are both very reasonable people.

As for me, I freely admit to being a mess. I'd started being impossible at thirteen, and at sixteen I was still there. I wasn't impossible all the time, just often enough to keep mother off balance. I was never a problem in school; I enjoyed it. Most of the time I was a very pleasant, reasonable girl, but every so often I'd pull a wing-ding. Like lying when I didn't have anything to lie about, just for the sake of lying. Or saying I was in one place when I was really in another and it didn't matter a bit anyway where I was. Junk like that. Also threatening to run away about once a month.

Running away had an enormous attraction for me, and after Dick really pulled out and did it—well! I had all sorts of visions. Don't ask me why I pulled this stuff, I haven't the slightest idea. It just seemed the in thing to do. Everybody did it.

And then this particular night something happened. I stayed out too late and then decided to run away, for no good reason. Or really any reason. The later it got the more I decided it would be a marvelous thing to do. I was at a girl friend's house where I was going to hide out until the morning and then take off. But her mother found me, called my mother, gave me aspirin and a tranquilizer, which I didn't need, and sent me home in a taxi with explicit directions to the driver.

In the meantime though, as the hours crawled along from 7 to 8 to 10 to 1 A.M., my mother had gone full circle from wrath to worry, to a complete recap of her life and "Where had she gone wrong?" and back to full-blown fury again. Of course she hadn't done *anything* wrong! But that's the one thing parents can't grasp. They think they must have done something wrong, or it doesn't make sense. They don't see that nothing has to make sense any more.

While she was worrying, she also investigated my room, which is something she never did, because my parents have a big thing about privacy. There she found a list that looked like a running-away list to her. Of course it wasn't. It was simply a list, like you make lists—but the top item was cigarettes. And she found lots of packages of cigarettes in my bureau, and I'm sure all this must have distressed her terribly because it didn't coincide at all with the way she had decided to handle the cigarette problem.

She had figured that if she said, "*Smoke!* Go ahead —I'm not going to stop you!" why then of course I'd lose all interest in smoking. Not so. But then parents never understand things like that. It's just handy for us they think that way, because then you can always come back at them with, "You *said* it was all right!" Usually they're terribly pained by this but they have nothing to say, really. They *can't* say anything or they'll be inconsistent, so they generally smile weakly and wonder where to go from there.

Oh well, the whole thing is like that. I mean all of life is like that with parents, and as long as you can look at it like a game, it's okay. The only really dangerous times are the ones like this one was, when you know you've pushed them too far, and they're wild with frustration and all the unexpressed things they've always wanted to express but didn't because they were trying to be good parents. All you can do at a time like that is be quiet and wait for it to blow over.

Unfortunately, there were two of them there when I got home. And even though they never really agree on how to handle things, when they're together they pretend to agree, for my sake of course, and the force of this pretended togetherness is pretty wild. The fact that they're both *trying* so hard makes it even worse. It's practically Wagnerian.

My father was sitting right there waiting for me. He is not tall but sometimes he looks tall. Actually he's only five feet eight. He has putty-colored hair that starts way back off his forehead because he's lost so much of it, and a thin, David Niven sort of face. Sometimes he has a mustache which grows in blond, but he always gets unhappy with it after a couple of days and shaves it off. He looks terrible in a beard (which he's tried) but perfectly marvelous in Dick's Australian bush hat, which I made him put on once. When I saw him in it I couldn't believe this gorgeous movie type was my father. That's what hair would ordinarily do for him, you see.

He usually wasn't home when I arrived late. He works as a waiter in the evenings, but of course he isn't a waiter at all. He's the last person in the world you could imagine ever being a waiter. He's actually an entrepreneur who's never quite managed to keep any of his enterprises going. He's a product of the depression and World War Two and only had one year of college and didn't become a doctor or lawyer or engineer or anything that's useful in this society. He had an elegant childhood before the crash, and even for a time after. So he's a dreamer of big dreams and that's what makes him an entrepreneur.

In between all these projects that come and go, like theaters, restaurants, bars, politics, inventions, games, TV shows, schemes to save the world, etc., he works as a waiter to make money. His hobby is eating. Really. Which is quite crazy when you look at him because he's so thin. He won't work anyplace that isn't gourmet because he wants his pâté and frogs legs once a day. And even before that, for lunch, he almost always eats out in another gourmet establishment on his American Express card.

I think that the worst thing in the world that could happen to my father would be to lose his American Express card. He carries it around in a little plastic folder in a special place. The rest of his papers are a mess. His pockets are always filled with bits of scribbled numbers and names and schemes for more projects. But one thing that he always knows *where it is* and can produce instantly is his American Express card.

The things you can charge on an American Express card are simply incredible! You can eat, go to hotels, fly anywhere in the world, buy clothes, have your hair done—it's really amazing. My mother once got so upset at all these possibilities that she demanded one too. She told my father that he seemed to regard his card as a passport to freedom, and therefore she needed one too, for her sense of security. I guess he understood, because he got her one. She tucked it away somewhere, never used it, but somehow she did look more secure. Not smug. Just secure. I frankly think she considered it like those long hatpins ladies used to stick in their purses. Or like a gun in a drawer. It was mother's secret weapon.

"Everybody else is dropping out, and believe me, it's just about my turn!" said my mother. "Overbrook, I hope you're hearing this message. You'd better back me up in this."

Yes, my father's name is actually Overbrook. He's Overbrook Almon Andrews the Third, but mother never calls him that except in moments of stress. It's usually just "Brook."

He was sitting on the Windsor chair next to our drop-leaf table, hands clasped between his knees, leaning forward a little to give an impression of extreme interest and "father concurs" in the proceedings. I don't think he heard half of what she said, because in the middle of this he took out one of those little papers and made notes. But he tried to look as if he heard, and every so often bellowed assorted warnings. "Listen to your mother!" . . . "I absolutely agree!" . . . "There'll be no more talk of running away!"

Of course what mother left out of all this was just as important as what she put in. She was really including my *father's* periodic and unpredictable disappearances. Every so often he would just sort of not show up for a couple of days because of one "project" or another. This was perfectly all right, or would have been, except that he usually forgot to call home and mother would wake up with an empty space next to her and panic. If he did remember, mother would get a call at something like 3 A.M. and could never get back to sleep. When he reappeared they would always argue about that, and it invariably ended with him saying one of two things: "I'm damned if I do, and damned if I don't!" or "Well, my dear, you can't have your cake and eat it too." That last remark would really infuriate mother.

She is the sort of person who should have married an Arabian-type man. The kind that knocks you around and puts you in your place, or locks you up in a harem with a veil over your face. Or even the kind of man who rides off into the wheat fields at dawn with a wave at the little gingham-clad figure standing at the farmhouse door. That would be mother, in an apron, sending up clouds of flour as she kneaded dough on the old rough-hewn table, and worked her knuckles to the bone from dawn to dusk. Something like that. She's really very feminine, sort of a cross between an Oriental slave and an American pioneer. But today's world doesn't allow her to be as feminine as she'd like to be, you see, so she has a problem.

My father has too. He was just made to go to Alaska in the gold rush, or start new businesses down in New Orleans when they used to do things like that, or be a big oil man. Junk like that. They're both horribly out of place in this century, and I think they both know it, although they won't admit it. They found each other, got married, and being nice people were absolutely determined to do their best. They do their utmost, their very, very utmost, to keep up with the times, and with each other. Because of that they are *extraordinarily* good parents, and that's where we run into so much trouble.

Dick and I were brought up on Spock and Gesell

and a wonderful balance of permissiveness-discipline, tremendous understanding, interest, vitamins, museums, walks, books, goldfish, love. And sometime recently—I suppose it was when Dick disappeared into that maze of dormitories—mother got the message. I'm sure father got it too, but he usually just thinks things while mother says them. That's a big part of her problem too. She wants someone else to say them for her, meaning my father, but nobody does, so she's stuck with all this "bringing things out into the open" and it leaves her feeling pressured and unfeminine. Anyway, when she got the message it was like stars exploding around the room.

"Don't you see what the problem is, Brook? Do you know why we can't do anything for our children? We're too nice. We're too reliable. Maybe we love them too much. They're too sure of us. We are far too understanding! Look at poor Dick . . ."

Even in the middle of this she could still say "poor Dick"! It's really amazing how they can't get away from understanding.

"What does poor Dick have to rebel against? Nothing! And it's a natural instinct. Kids have to rebel, I think. Do you agree? Brook, are you listening to me? Do you realize that there are millions of kids dropping out, and millions of parents like us? I don't think affluence has that much to do with it—I think a great part is *us*. Too loving, too intelligent, too nice and understanding. If they're so well understood from the very beginning, what chance do they ever have to fight for understanding—or anything—in themselves?"

Then her eyes widened as if she were seeing a vision. "Brook, if they all get tired of it and ever see what's happened, the next generation may reverse the trend. A wave of Puritanism may sweep the world. And that might be just as bad. You could see toddlers in pinafores and high collars standing in lines at water fountains, growing up to say, 'Yes, Ma'am' and 'No, Sir.' Oh dear, Brook! If this generation has the benefit of all our experience, and we've gone too far, the next may just swing violently in the other direction. And it'll go on forever, with that pendulum swinging, swinging." She dropped into a chair, exhausted.

I think it was this message though, this new "understanding" of hers, that precipitated the final event. She saw that there was really nowhere further to go. Everything was going to be the same. Dick might go back to school or he might not go back to school. It was out of her hands. She couldn't undo anything she'd done, or do anything she hadn't done. And anyway, they'd always been right in the middle. She could tell me not to smoke cigarettes but she knew I would anyway, and anything else that I really wanted. I could always approach her one way or the other because she was always ready to listen. I could appeal to past statements; or to her "understanding," or to her sense of fair play. I could make an issue out of anything or not make an issue, but it would wind up just the same. And if I really ran into a stone wall on anything, why then I could go to my father and appeal to his understanding or his sense of fair play. And he would talk to mother, and one way or the other it would always work out just the way I wanted. Dick and I had always handled things like that. It was really very simple. Our parents are MLU's. Middle-Liberal-Understanding, and we had been brought up in an atmosphere where everybody tried to understand everybody and do the right thing.

For instance, I am sixteen and I look about twenty-two. Mother is around forty and she looks about twenty-eight. This should have led us into one of those competitive mother-daughter clashes around this time, but mother is so understanding that of course it didn't happen. We talked about it, naturally, and there went another of those great growing-up experiences right down the drain!

She assured me that as I got older I would look younger. That's what happened to her. At eighteen she looked thirty, and it's absolutely true, because I've seen the pictures. So I stopped worrying about the way I look. If it didn't have a certain connotation, I'd say I looked voluptuous. Oh, I'll say it anyway. I have a sort of precocious child's mind in a vaudeville body which I keep trying to cover up. Would you believe that with all this I'd have *Jane* for a name? Plain old Jane!

I guess my name, and Dick's—which is really Richard—were our parents' reaction to their own names, Overbrook and Wanda. I mean, *nobody* is Overbrook and Wanda! And if they are, they sure don't have kids named Dick and Jane! The teachers in our private school really freaked on this, as Dick would say. They introduced us around to visiting parents as if we were a special joke. "We have a real Dick and Jane!" "Here are our Dick and Jane!" Very funny! Our parents didn't know what they were doing when they labeled us! They weren't even in the *Dick and Jane* generation. When they found out, through the school, they laughed and promptly named our goldfish "Spot."

Well anyway, I don't know what got into me that night, but when my mother started talking about running away herself, I just guffawed, I thought it was so funny. Then too, I was filled with this sense of power from having planned to run away myself, and I was bouncing back and forth between a vision of myself as a flower girl in the East Village or as a waitress in some little hamlet upstate, passing myself off as twenty-one or even twenty-five, and being my old familiar self, Jane, at home with my parents. I didn't know quite where I was or where I wanted to be, so I got hysterical with laughter, and the more I laughed the more mother's expression changed. She looked weird!

Then just the day after that my father pulled one of his disappearing stunts, and didn't remember to call until 4:30 A.M. He had gone to Albany on some deal that had come up very quickly about introducing a bill in the State Legislature to legalize gambling in discotheques, which, if they got it introduced and passed, would give him a job. To me it sounded as if he would then become a bookie, but I don't know. Whatever it was, it was just the sort of thing that was always coming up.

Mother never got back to sleep after he called, so when the post card arrived from Dick that morning, she was already drawn, harassed, and exhausted. All she needed was the news that he had now skipped altogether. He wasn't even hanging around the college any more; he'd hitched to Southern California and was living on the beach with some surfing types. He didn't even say which beach. "Real gas, this. Sun's great! Hello to the squirt." No hello to mother, no information about how he was eating, what he was living on, not even a "Don't worry, I'm okay."

You see, we are all so absolutely certain in our family of all this ground swell of understanding, that everybody loves everybody, even if nobody particularly likes anybody or likes them sometimes and not others. that there are certain things we just never remember to say. Like *"Love, don't worry, I'm okay."*

Mother shoved the card at me, went to the bookcase, took out her copy of *Karma Yoga,* and went to her room. I never knew whether this yoga business was an escape for mother or something real. In light of what was about to happen, I guess it's real enough. Also, not only has she been reading it for such a long time, but she's often gotten irritated by it too. I remember her putting down a book on some Eastern philosophy one day, and saying to my father, "Oh! Why must they keep using that word!"

"What word?" he asked.

"Ineffable!" she sputtered. "It's always ineffable sweetness, ineffable joy, ineffable ecstasy. It makes everything sound so ineffably *easy*—all honey and roses and cream. If it weren't for that word, I think I might like to go to India."

Mother has worked pretty hard at everything, including understanding, all her life. And in spite of her basic femininity, she isn't exactly the type you could imagine drowning in a pool of lotus blossoms. She expects things to be hard work—even Eastern religion.

Now comes the astounding and unbelievable part. The very next day mother disappeared. One minute she was there, washing up the dishes. Then she got dressed in a suit, wrote a little note, and walked out. She walked out with the clothes on her back and a purse. That's absolutely all! Six days later we got a post card from her. She had somehow overcome the "ineffable" hurdle, and was in India—in an ashram. In case you don't know, an ashram is some kind of a special retreat for study and meditation.

She had gotten there on her American Express card, of course.

I tell you, there is practically nothing that you can't do with one of those American Express cards.

Two

Mother's first note, her "kitchen note," said, "Need a little rest and will be gone for a while. Am sure you can both manage. I'll be in touch later. Wanda."

How about that! No "love," not even "Mother." Just "Wanda." If the rest of us forgot, at least mother always signed her notes "love, Mother." *Always*. That note threw me. Of course we expected her back momentarily. We thought she had gone to a hotel for a night or two, something like that. The longer she was gone the worse my father looked. By the third day he was really distracted, thin-lipped and everything. Besides being uneasy about mother, I thought I knew what else was bothering him. And sure enough I was right. He was worried about the American Express card! Since he had procured it for her, he was responsible. When that post card arrived air mail from *India* I thought he'd faint.

"Arrived yesterday by Pan Am through A.E.!"

The exclamation point after A.E. told the whole story.

"To ashram today, will write if I can. Have fun."

She didn't even *sign* that one! No word about where she was going, where the ashram was, how long she'd be there. And she didn't even say "will write *when* I can." "Will write *if* I can." Wow!

I have never seen my father so befuddled in his life.

I got the impression he couldn't believe she had done it. By Pan American—on American Express! It wasn't the interest in India or the ashram that puzzled him. It was the fact that it was done. She had dared!

As long as I can remember, mother had been reading Eastern philosophy. *Her* mother was a Christian Scientist who slipped from that into Unity, which in turn, I guess, set mother up for this interest. My father's parents were Quakers, but he had sort of drifted away and Dick and I were both baptized in the Episcopal Church, and then never saw it again. This was to appease both grandmothers who wanted us saved *somehow*. Dick was very unhappy that he wasn't an official Quaker, because then he wouldn't have been eligible for the draft. But that Episcopal certificate sort of doomed him, and it was a little late in the day to claim serious Quaker sympathies. A few months before, on his eighteenth birthday, he and my father had a rather large argument about that, because he had to go and register for the draft. Why hadn't father foreseen this? How come the *Episcopal Church?* Well, it was just that at baptism time St. Michael's was around the corner, and that's how it all happened.

Oh well, this entire thing is typically MLU. I mean the religious mix-up. The only one in our family who seemed to have any sort of serious interest in anything was my mother. But being just old Eastern stuff and strange books, it was sort of pooh-poohed, and regarded as mother's little hobby. In general, except for me, it was ignored. I had gone into her books somewhat, but I'll get to that later.

We live on the Upper East Side of New York City, by the East River, and not in one of those huge new slick apartment buildings or anything like that. We are near the end of a side street, near Carl Schurz Park and Gracie Mansion, where the mayor lives. We're in one of those old houses that have been converted into small apartments, but we happen to have a five-room apartment on the ground floor. It's a little like a railroad flat in that one room leads into another. But it's somehow larger. Our living room looks onto the street, and in back of that is mother and daddy's room, cleverly made separate by a floor-to-ceiling bookcase with a door cut into it. This makes a small hall as you go back. Next comes Dick's room, which is quite open, containing bunk beds, a desk, shelves, working space and chairs. He used to make it private with a folding screen, but since he's been away at school, it's been used as a den or study or TV room. In back of that is a huge kitchen, with a small room next to it, which is mine, and outside, a postage-stamp-sized garden. The kitchen windows and my window look out on the garden which has one tree, a small playing and planting space, and a nice round wrought-iron table with chairs for eating outside. Our whole apartment runs back along a little cement walk bordered with grass and some bushes, between our building and the next. I think this is what makes it seem larger, because each room has a side window with light.

Once upon a time these old houses weren't even heated, and people had to supply their own kerosene stoves. My mother and father found the place when it was like that, just before Dick was born. Then it was rehabilitated, like most of the houses in this area, and we now have steam heat and peepholes. When the landlord did all that, he also raised all the rents and evicted most of the old people who lived in the building. They couldn't afford the new prices, but mother and daddy stayed. They had moved in when the rent was something like fifty dollars a month and, even with the increase, they couldn't find anything better. Besides that, they had really fixed the place up, and didn't want to leave their creative effort.

Sometimes, though, my father seems dismayed that the rent isn't still $50. He doesn't believe in rent. There are several other things he doesn't believe in either. Like taxes, doctors, and telephone bills. He loathes telephone bills, even though, due to his projects, he's responsible for most of the calls. He's really mixed up. He uses all these modern conveniences like mad and then complains bitterly at the cost. He had this very old-fashioned idea, you see, that you build your own house, and own the property, and that there shouldn't be any taxes on it at all, and that the income tax amendment should be repealed. All doctors should be white-haired gents who treat everybody either for nothing or for $3.00 a throw. This is what I mean, partly, about his being in the wrong century. All his bills mount up, always, except for the American Express. That one he pays promptly, on the dot! In fact I sometimes have the feeling that he can't wait to get it, and that he actually worries about it until it comes and the check has gone off.

Before he went to work that day when the post card arrived, we sat together in the living room and father said nervously, "We'd better talk about this, Jane. Your mother's in India."

"I know." Naturally I knew. The card was to both of us. I think he said it out loud to try and tell himself it was really true.

"Dick is out in California."

"I know." This was the same thing, I think. He was trying to get a grip on the whereabouts of his family; kind of trying to drag all of us into place geographically. I even saw him glance at our globe of the world on a stand in a corner of the room.

"She's really dropped out," he said, looking at me as if I could tell him it wasn't true. I just nodded.

"I don't know when she'll be back," he said. It was really a question, and in that moment, honest to goodness, I knew what it felt like to be a woman. Here was this poor man, addressing me, the only other feminine member of the family, in hopes that I could tell him something about women. The way women's minds work. But *I* didn't know! I was as surprised as he was.

"What are we going to do?" he asked.

"*I* don't know!"

He looked at me for a moment, as if giving up all hope of any feminine advice, and seemed to recall that I was only sixteen. He planted his hands firmly on his knees and leaned forward. "Have any bills come in?"

"No," I said, knowing quite well what he meant.

"Well, we don't know where to reach her," he started, sort of talking to himself. "She may write again, but I also have the impression she may not. If she doesn't write, I don't know how we can locate her."

Suddenly I got mad. And scared, too. The way he was talking, it sounded as if she really might not come back. And how could he be so ineffectual! Why didn't he just take over! There was mother gone, and here were we, and all he could think of was how he couldn't get in touch with her! Besides, even if we could get to her, how was she supposed to solve any problems all the way from India?

"Well," I said flippantly, "you could always contact Interpol."

After that we didn't talk about it for a few days. I stayed pretty close to the house, because I didn't know what else to do, and then we did receive a letter from her. A one-page hurried scrawl on one of those Par Avion flimsy sheets. It said absolutely nothing although my father seemed to think it said everything.

> Dear Brook and Jane,
> It's wonderful here. Nothing ineffable! Rest and work. Sure you won't mind the bill after all those lunches. Also sure everyone's old enough to take care of themselves. You can take care of each other. If Dick writes again say hello. Have no idea at all how long I'll be here. Have to go—I'm terribly busy. By the way, Indian girls at sixteen are really mature young women. Incredible. Take care,
>
> > Love,
> P.S. If someone's expiring you can cable through American Express office, Bombay.

She hadn't even signed her name to this one, although it did say "Love." I guess being in an ashram she would feel like saying love. She did include the fact that we could contact her if someone was at death's door, but outside of that the whole tone of that letter drove both of us wild, for different reasons.

My father went blue and tried not to show me how it affected him. He was furious! It was that remark about all his lunches. That, and the horribly *free* quality of the thing. With me, it was that remark about Indian girls at sixteen. It made me so upset I couldn't stand it, but I couldn't stop thinking about it, either. What did she mean! How *dare* she imply that I wasn't mature, or whatever she was implying. And on top of that, *she'd* walked out! If I weren't a mature young woman, how dare she desert me if there were something further she had to do with me! I was *her* responsibility! On the other hand, she hadn't really deserted me; she'd just gone for a "rest" and turned me over to my father. But we didn't know for how long. And he couldn't take care of the situation. Or could he? I didn't know. And, at the same time, she was implying that I was old enough to be responsible for myself, or that we could be responsible for each other. Oh, it was simply horrible!

And the free tone got me too. I couldn't stand it! Who did she think she was, anyway? I mean, it might as well have been a letter from *Dick!*

I have never been in such a state in my life. If she had written an explanatory letter, like she was sorry but she would wind up in the giggle house if she didn't have a rest . . . That kind of thing, begging for our understanding and approval. If she'd even done more description of the trip, or how she felt, or asked how we were, or given instructions. Yes! If she'd only included something like, "Remember to tell the milkman one less." Or, "Jane's dress is at the cleaners." Anything like that. But she didn't. She sounded so free, so—*ineffably cool*—that it almost killed me. I felt like sending her a cable saying I was dying.

Then I got mad and decided to prove that I wasn't trustworthy or responsible at all. I really would run away this time. I'd go join Dick on the beach. Except that I didn't have any money and didn't even know which beach he was on. Then I had a vision of my father all alone in the apartment with all of us gone and had a wild thought that if that happened he might take off too—go prospecting in Venezuela, or join a monastery himself. And if the whole thing collapsed like that nobody would have anything to go back to. No apartment, no clothes, nothing. I had this wild vision of the whole world crumbling, all the kids taking off, all the parents splitting. What a mess!

If only I had an American Express card myself! I could have taken off for a few days and sent father a wire saying I'd be right back. Just to keep him there so I'd have something to go back to. I really had visions of that—lying around a plush pool down in Puerto Rico, pretending I was a twenty-five-year-old divorcée and getting into lots of trouble. I don't know why, just to prove something.

My father and I stared at each other for several days around this time and didn't say much. I went to school every morning—there was only one week left before summer vacation—and I came right home in the afternoon. He actually waited for me and gave up his late A.E. lunches. That was the only good thing about this whole weird time. He would cook these crazy lunches for himself at home, mackerel, anchovies, white wine, stuff like that, and then leave it for me for my dinner. He went off to work just at six and I stayed home every single night and watched television. I couldn't read, for the first time in my life.

I usually read *everything*, including matchbook covers. And then I always forget everything I've read within a day, although sometimes something stays with me. It may be that in all this reading I'm really searching to find out what I already know, because that's the only part I can remember. Once, for instance, when I had looked into mother's books, a lot of it was like something I already knew, and even remembered. But there was also a lot I didn't understand, and most of it seemed to say, "Wait." I felt I was too young. I suppose this would have been the perfect time to investigate those books again, but I couldn't go near them.

I watched so much television I began to feel sick. I even watched *cartoons* in the afternoon! I saw a little kid running around in front of our house one day pretending to be Road Runner, going "beep-beep" up and down. I knew exactly how he felt! It was such a wild, crazy thing that I actually tried it myself, all the way from the front room to the garden. "Beep-beep" all the way!

It didn't help a bit, and that was the moment, I think, when I did what you call "putting away childish things." That was my last stab at being a kid. This "beep-beep" coming out loud you see, instead of just in my imagination, was a terrific shock. I *heard* the whole bit. I was being a child for my mother's benefit and she wasn't even there!

There was something else involved, too, in being alone after school like that. I was having a peculiar time about the matter of friends. My very best friend, the girl I'd grown up with, who lived around the corner, had moved away last year. Her parents were like my parents and everybody was very buddy-buddy. Her father happened to work in an advertising agency, but he hated it, and was always trying to get out by dreaming up some deal, just like my father. In fact, they often dreamed up projects together. She also had a brother, older than Dick, who went into the peace movement very early, and when draft time came they all pulled out and went to Canada! They had very understanding parents too, you see. Well, everybody lost out then. My father lost Warren, his project buddy, I lost Mary, Dick lost Carl, and my mother lost Mary's mother, Amy, who understood her completely because they lived exactly the same lives. Both of them had rather expensive, private-school, elegant backgrounds, and both found themselves in what I guess you call "genteel poverty." Working part-time, saving for private schools and college, never having quite enough rest or quite enough money for dentists and clothes and stuff.

Mother suggested that I bring some other girls to the house, which I did, and I even started to be rather popular in school as other girls began to catch up with me. But somehow I never found another Mary. I was sort of "between best friends" when all this happened, and there was no one I really wanted to take into my confidence. It didn't really bother me; I had no doubt at all that a best friend would come along some day. Mother always said, "You can't *make* things happen, Jane. You'll be better off if you let them happen."

But I couldn't stand thinking about things mother had told me because I knew she had tried to bring me up so well. I didn't understand anything; why I bugged my mother, why I was a mess, why Dick had skipped, why everybody was on grass. *I* would have been probably, if I could stand the smell. But the smell really made me ill, so my only gesture could be cigarettes. I didn't understand why I had to have cigarettes, why everybody had to have something, why everybody I knew was going so wild, why my father was pathological about his American Express card, why my mother had dropped out.

There's one place in New York that I've always

found very comforting. The Battery. Nobody knows that I go there, and I don't know anybody else who goes there. I can be completely alone. One Sunday after mother left I lied to my father—this was a good honest lie for a good purpose—and told him I was going to the movies. I went down to Battery Park to be alone.

Three

The way I go around alone is like this. I wear sneakers, slacks to hide my legs, a baggy shirt, and a sloppy, shapeless, tan raincoat. Then I pin my hair back in an old-fashioned bun at the back of my neck, tight behind the ears, and I put on a pair of imitation horn-rimmed eyeglasses that are just plain glass. I picked them up at the dime store for just this purpose. I also bought a fake gold wedding ring for the same reason. That usually takes care of it, but if I have any doubts, I add a shredded old scarf and tie it around my head. I am completely unrecognizable! I can disappear into any old crowd like that. I look kind of like a poor school teacher or old maid, sort of like a peasant, or a beer-drinking young wife who's got an unemployed husband. But the main thing is I'm practically invisible.

It's the only way, because if I get dressed up or even look normal, I can't go a block without something happening. People *look* and you have no privacy. The worst ones of all are the construction men. They not only look, they whistle and make remarks. It's nothing to worry about because they whistle at everybody. I've seen them whistling at my mother. But it's irritating.

I got off the subway and walked over to the water

where you can lean against the rail and look at the Statue of Liberty and watch the ferryboats and tugboats and all the harbor traffic. It was not a very nice day; it was kind of misty and gray, which suited my mood completely. Nevertheless the park was filled with people, there were lots of kids running around up and down the walk, and some old guy had a portable record player on a bench that was spinning out old tunes from the 1920's. "Yes! We Have No Bananas" . . . "In My Merry Oldsmobile" . . . "Happy Days Are Here Again."

When he put on "Happy Days Are Here Again" I thought I'd die. It was practically my mother's favorite song! Every time she felt in a bad mood, she'd start singing it. It was even before her time, but I'd heard it as long as I could remember. Sometimes she even sang it at bedtime!

I moved up the walk away from him, but that music kept following me. Everybody else seemed to like it, particularly some little kids, so he put it on again and turned up the volume. Oh, was that weird! I stood there looking at the Statue of Liberty with that music in my ears, trying to visualize my mother in the ashram. Pretty soon I began to visualize my mother as the Statue of Liberty. There was some terrible connection between all of it—and I didn't want to understand it!

I took out my cigarettes and had two real quick. I ground the butts under my feet I was so mad. Usually I just flip them. What I wanted to do was turn my mother off. She was part of everything I didn't understand: dropouts, India. She was part of the youth movement! Then it occurred to me that half the authority—if there was any authority—was gone. I was pretty sure I could talk my father into almost anything. I already had! I was *here,* not at the movies! Here was all the freedom I could ever want, to do just about anything!

I looked at the Statue of Liberty some more and tried to pretend it was me. I wished somebody would do something horrible with her—stick a cigarette in her mouth, or why not a pot party up in the lamp?

The old fellow put the song on again, and that did it. I decided to go on the ferry.

The sign in the ferry building just killed me. In 1970 it still said FIVE CENTS for a ferry ride. I figured it was about the only thing left in the world for only five cents and it always made me feel better. The ferries are nice, too. They're a loud mustard-orangey color, trimmed in royal blue. My problem on the ferries is that I never know where to go. The trip doesn't take long enough, and I want to be everywhere and see everything. On a clear day the colors in the harbor and the feeling of space are terrific. But even on a misty day it's great. I suppose the only place where I'd be really happy would be on top of the boat, in the captain's house. But nobody is allowed up there, and the upper decks always have too many people. I usually scuttle around from port to starboard, on all the decks, and never light anywhere. But on this day I stayed down on the lowest deck, where the cars are ferried over in the center section. On either side are two long smoking sections. And right in back, at the stern, you can stand practically over the water and get hit by spray and watch the seagulls following the boat. I stayed down there and had more cigarettes, and in between went out to watch the water. Everybody else seemed to be upstairs, watching the Statue of Liberty.

When you get to Staten Island, you can't just stay

on the boat to return to Manhattan. You have to get off, walk all the way around, and put another nickel in the turnstile to come back. But at that point I just didn't feel like coming back. For the first time in days I was beginning to feel a little better. Being on the water always washes things out of my mind. I was feeling sort of empty and loose and wanted to stay that way. Then I saw the sign for the trains to Tottenville.

I knew that Tottenville was at the other side of Staten Island, but I had no idea it was also at the end of the world. I just felt crazy enough to take a ride out there. It cost only thirty-five cents each way. So I bought a ticket and walked down to this gloomy shed where the train was waiting. Train? I don't know what to call it. It was two ancient cars, hooked together, grimy and creaky, with a network of wire on the windows, and wicker seats with brass handles on the ends. The seats were clean and the brass was shining, but the rest of the train looked as if it hadn't been touched since Roosevelt was President. Franklin Delano, that is.

The conductor looked like a small Santa Claus with round red cheeks, and he didn't walk, he bounced. He was right out of the New Deal, too, or even earlier. I've never seen anybody so cheerful in my life, and it was really strange. This happy, sunshiny conductor in that dismal, dirty shed.

We started off. There were only three other people in the front car, and nobody in the rear car. We jerked and rolled and creaked, and then went evenly, and then jerked again.

I'd never been anywhere on Staten Island except right there in St. George where the ferries come in. Once we visited some people who lived on a hill right near the ferry buildings, but other than that Staten Island was a mystery to me. I always thought that if you left the main part, you'd find something like suburbia or pretty farms among rolling hills, something like that. Well, I couldn't have been more wrong. Right there along the railroad tracks at least, it all looked like a huge desolation.

We pulled out of the shed and ran alongside shacks and old ferry slips and bleak boatyards, then stopped at something resembling a junkyard, and then went on from there. I wish I could give you this picture. This gloomy day, this sunny conductor, "Happy Days Are Here Again" still playing in the back of my head —and that train ride straight back into the 1920's and 1930's. There were all these little towns out of another century. Grasmere, Grant City, New Dorp . . . *New Dorp!* Little, toy streets, shabby old houses with old-fashioned back yards, a few pretty, shaded streets where the trees met together and the houses were a little newer. But even where there were stretches of planned "doggy-boxes," everything looked faded and weedy and downright tacky. It was all so ancient. Then, when you saw something that looked modern, like a big new school that just shricked with efficiency, it was still like the kind of modern thing they did back in the 30's. Not *now!* And along with this went the conductor, bouncing up and down the aisle, grinning at everybody, helping people off and on, and pulling a train whistle that sounded like it should have been in the movies!

Then the conductor got so busy talking to someone that he forgot to stop at a station where two passengers wanted to get off, and we went right past. Then—this is unbelievable—*he stopped the train and backed it up to let them off!* And afterwards came chortling down the aisle singing, "And this is the way we run our railroad!"

On top of that, I actually saw him, with my own

eyes, tying a note around an umbrella that some man had forgotten. He knew exactly when that man was going to get the train again, and when he could retrieve his umbrella! I didn't think this sort of thing had happened since the 1890's, or anyway outside of British movies.

By the time we got to Tottenville I was the last person on the train. I guess almost nobody travels to Tottenville during the day except the train and the conductors, and being alone, I just knew he would talk to me if I made one motion. So I huddled against the window and wouldn't look at him. We pulled into the station alongside a covered ramp, I got up fast, asked him quickly how often the train ran, found out it was every twenty minutes "more or less," and then I fled.

I ran down the cement ramp under the shed, hoping to find something familiar in Tottenville. You know, a candy store, a movie house, a pizza parlor, something to let me know I was still in New York in this century. There were weeds around the railroad tracks, another blue Staten Island Rapid Transit train waiting to make the return journey, and a decrepit old station booth at the end. And, as I came round it, right in front of me, was *nowhere*.

A sidewalk, a street, and nothing beyond except more weeds, a jungle of poison ivy, straggly bushes, and the murky water around Staten Island. The ruined, half-burned skeleton of an old ferry house loomed up from the end of a pier. Across the channel were smoke stacks belching from the factories in New Jersey, all covered with a smoggy gray mist. The sidewalk where I stood led up a hill and, I guessed, into Tottenville proper. But all I could see up there, beyond some old buildings on my left, were

more little houses and trees. I could almost feel that
conductor breathing down my neck, so I walked away
fast, with the long raincoat flapping halfway down
my slacks. He was like one of those conductors you
find in science fiction stories who come up and offer
you a ticket to somewhere back in time, or off to another planet. Sometimes they come up to you with
these cute, cherubic faces, but they're really evil people. You can get into a real mess with conductors in
strange stories.

I walked past the old buildings to the top of the
hill and looked down the intersection of streets. Nothing, in any direction, except more trees and antique
houses. I crossed the street, thinking I might walk
down toward the water, and there, in a little house
at the end of a vacant lot, I saw a neon sign in the
window. For a second I thought I'd found something
really twentieth century. It was a beer sign and it was
this bar. I'd never been in a bar alone in my life, only with my parents after the theater. But with that
neon sign, and other posters, it looked *normal,* so I
opened the faded green door and stepped in.

Nowhere again! This bar was unbelievable. It could
have been out in the middle of an Iowa wilderness or
at some tiny crossroads in Indiana. There was an old
grizzled bartender, cards and advertisements leaning
askew against the bar mirror and all over the walls, a
big pool table, an ancient juke box, a telephone
booth, some tables, and hanging from a corner, a
black bird in a cage. The bartender had his sleeves
rolled up with rubber bands! I noticed that because
he was just taking a bottle down when I walked in,
and his arms were up. He turned around with the
bottle, saw me come in, and I marched right past him
to the end of the bar where I saw a LADIES' ROOM sign.

That's when I took all this in, including some people sitting at the bar, and one lone guy at a table in the back, next to a window.

The ladies' room had one of those hard-to-close doors with no lock. It was so tiny I could hardly turn around. Maybe once it was a closet. The light was bad, too, so I couldn't see myself very well in the mirror. But I figured the way I looked, and felt, I could have been thirty—forty even. So I marched out and sat down at the bar. There wasn't anything else to do, really. I didn't know why I'd come out here, I could hardly figure out where I was, and the last thing I wanted was to go out and see any more of old Tottenville!

That bar was really something. It was so old it almost seemed to tip toward me where I sat. On a shelf in back there was an ancient, ornate, gilded cash register, standing in front of a mirror. And above the mirror, framed like it was enshrined, was that famous photograph of the guys planting the flag on Iwo Jima.

Someone had put on the juke box and it suddenly began to play "Deep in the Heart of Texas!" Sitting there at the bar, I got sort of scared. If I ordered a Coke, the bartender might start to wonder, I thought. I really wanted a Coke, but I figured I looked like the sort of person who would automatically order beer. I hate beer! All this went very fast. I thought if I ordered a beer first, then I could order a Coke next time.

There were three pople down at the end of the bar near the street. A blowsy woman with red hair, a guy who looked like a truckdriver, and an older man who was so drunk he could hardly lift his glass. All of a sudden this crazy voice filled the room, "A slip of the lip might sink a ship! Rat-a-tat-tat-tat-tat!"

Nobody paid any attention! But I literally froze on the stool, it was so eerie. The voice went off again with the same words in the same tone, and then I realized it was the *bird!* Oh, wow, I was ready to leave, what with that and Iwo Jima. But just then the bartender came over to me.

"Beer, please," I said quickly. Then I wished I hadn't said "please," because I didn't *look* like the sort of person who would, but he didn't seem to notice. He just drew me a glass of beer. And it was right then that all the trouble started.

The old drunk heard me. First he leaned way over the bar to take a look at me, splashing his drink all over; then he practically fell off the stool trying to get off, and weaved his way down to where I sat. Oh, was he a creepy character. It wouldn't have been so bad if he were really unshaven and toothless, but he wasn't. He was just in-between. About fifty-five, I guess, and dressed all right, in a suit and tie. He actually had an almost kind, fatherly face that looked as if it had all sorts of other things in mind. His expression was sharp and repulsive. He must have been really desperate to take a look at me—I mean, you could hardly *see* me, I was so covered up—but he was so drunk maybe he didn't see anything. I think he had false teeth, because his smile was so horrible and even, and maybe a toupee, because his hair came too far forward.

He sloshed his drink all over my raincoat when he tried to put the glass down on the bar, and then pulled out his handkerchief and tried to wipe me off. I jumped and edged away. I really wanted to move to another stool, but I was nervous because I didn't know what someone like "me" should ordinarily do in that situation. So I laughed, pretending it was the sort of thing that happened all the time, while I tried to wave him off. The bartender frowned and looked as if he might step in at any minute, as this creep kept mumbling at me and tried to get his arm around my shoulder. I was about to duck and run at that point when the young guy from the table walked over, pushed himself between the drunk and me, and ordered himself a beer. The drunk got very sullen and mad, so this fellow between us said to me, "Oh why don't you go over to a table and have your drink."

He wasn't trying to pick me up, he didn't even say come to *his* table, but I did anyway. I sat down with him because I knew that character would follow me if I didn't. We left him at the bar, hanging onto it, and sat down together.

The red-haired woman jumped up from her stool, laughing, and went to the juke box. The next thing I heard was Frank Sinatra singing, "I'll Never Smile Again."

Well, I think I would have cracked up altogether then and there if it hadn't been for this young guy. I had an impulse to run over and look at the juke box myself, but I already knew I wasn't going to find anything reassuring like the Cream or Creedence Clearwater. Not on your life! I just knew those records hadn't been changed in twenty or thirty years. It wasn't that I didn't like Frank Sinatra; I like all kinds of music. But the whole thing was too much! So I stared at the guy sitting across the table, and gradually he came into focus.

He was the only understandable thing in the whole place, now that I really looked at him. He looked like people I knew. I mean, he could have been walking down East End Avenue, certainly 86th Street. He

could have gone to Columbia or lived in the Village
or been in California—he was just about like that.
There was something a little different about him, but
in general he looked very familiar. He had longish
dark-brown hair with mild sideburns, and really big
dark brown eyes. He was medium height and build,
a little stocky, and he had great hands. Terrific hands.
Long fingers, but not too thin, and the fingernails
weren't either too clean or too dirty. I'm always suspicious of people who have really clean or really dirty
fingernails. His were just right.

His outfit was funny though. It was kind of woods-
man-ish, and I hadn't seen that around in a long time.
A red plaid shirt with dungarees, and a corduroy
jacket thrown over the back of his chair. I wondered
about that, so I looked under the table and saw he
had boots. Big black high suede ones, with pointed
toes, and that was strange. They'd really been out for
a while, you know? I couldn't figure out his age because he had one of those strong, high cheek-boned
faces that could have been anything. It was sort of in-
between square and round, and he had a very gentle
mouth that didn't go with everything else. His eyes
weren't gentle; they were sort of hard and mysterious,
big as they were. I thought he was terribly good-looking, and he could have been twenty-five or nineteen;
I just couldn't tell.

Sitting there with him was kind of funny, when you
think about it, because what with my glasses and scarf
and old raincoat, he must have thought he was being
real nice to a thirty-year-old slob. He smiled at me,
and I wondered if I should go to the ladies' room
and let down my hair and everything. It wouldn't matter, because I'd still look old enough to be in a bar. I
really didn't know what to do.

Then the bird went off again, like he was competing with Frank Sinatra, and this guy laughed and said to me, "How do you like Tottenville?"

I felt like somebody had hit me over the head! He said *everything* in that question. It was as if he knew everything! I was so shocked that for a minute I couldn't speak. I glanced out the window at the vista of weeds and junk, murky water at the bottom of the hill, the burned ferry shed, the little brick station house with the sign saying RAPID TRANSIT LINES, and answered the first truthful thing that came to my mind.

"I don't know . . . I don't even know where Tottenville *is!*"

Four

Of course I was reading all sorts of things into his question. He probably didn't mean anything special. Maybe he thought I was from Tottenville, lived there, and he wondered how I liked it. But when I said I didn't know where it was, he looked as if *he'd* been hit over the head! That's how it all started. I saw him get this shock, and then a puzzled expression rippled all over his face as he looked at me.

Well! I sure wasn't much to look at! I saw him mentally trying to remove my scarf and glasses so he could place me in some category. His eyes traveled down to my hand with the wedding band. And that's when I knew I liked him, because even though he was obviously curious, he didn't say any of the obvious things like, "Where does your husband work?"

He only said, "I don't know where Tottenville is, either!" And he smiled, "Don't you want your beer?"

I hadn't touched it because the episode with the drunk had been so upsetting, and even to look at it made me ill. When I paused, he said, "Want something stronger?"

"Coke," I nodded.

He threw me another puzzled look, but went to the bar. Then I saw the drunk leaving. He was so stoned he couldn't even walk. He lurched, zigzagging, to the door, and fell against it. The truckdriver type got up to help him out, and a minute later I heard a car starting outside. The truckdriver sat down again, and everyone looked at the door, listening to that car. It was really scary, thinking of that guy trying to drive alone in that condition. My "friend" came back with the Coke shaking his head. "Friday and Saturday nights the kids pile over here from New Jersey and they all leave like that. Crazy. You can't get a drink over there until you're twenty-one."

He threw his leg over the chair and sat down. I could tell he was the sort of person who really likes to straddle a chair backwards and has to stop himself out in public. Lots of boys get into that at a certain age, and it made me wonder again how old he was. He'd said "until you're twenty-one," which seemed to imply that he might be under twenty-one. Maybe he was from New Jersey. You can see how intrigued I was, trying to figure all this out. I even noticed the way he set the Coke down in front of me, not carefully, but not slamming it, either. He just plunked it there, casually, and said, "Well—if you're not going to drink your beer—" and took it himself.

I was going to pull out some change for the Coke, but then I remembered that I hadn't yet paid for the beer, either. But he was going to drink it. I didn't know what to do.

This is the sort of thing that drives me crazy!

It can spoil everything! I knew I was going to be a nervous wreck until the money problem was straightened out. I wouldn't be able to think about anything else. So I pulled out a whole dollar and flipped it down as if it were a napkin, and left it between us on the table.

It seemed an okay thing to do because he didn't pay

any attention. In fact he seemed off somewhere, as if he'd forgotten me. It was the sort of place where you could easily sit with people and forget them. He jumped off the chair, fished out some change, and went to the juke box. This time it was "That Old Black Magic," and believe it or not, I knew that one too. If you don't know the music to this, forget it. But if you know the music, then you know the feeling. I'd heard a lot of this old stuff because my parents have a large record collection; it's all from their day.

My mother and father always said that this is the first generation to really know something about previous generations, thanks to records and movies and TV. They're right about that, too. Think of all those shows. Not only the 30's and 40's and 50's movies, but things like *The Little Rascals, Laurel and Hardy*, W. C. Fields films. Why I've even seen the Flash Gordon series! I remembered lots of old music, like "That Old Black Magic," from the 40's, just from seeing so many World War Two movies on TV. In fact World War Two seems kind of familiar to me, like home, there are so many movies about it. But then I guess one war is pretty much like another.

He seemed to know the music, too, because he was looking out the window and listening as if it meant something to him. He was very far away. I didn't want him to completely forget me, so first I took off my glasses and rubbed my eyes and blinked a lot, and yawned. You know, all that stuff you do when you want to look natural as if you don't wear glasses all the time, and you've suddenly realized you have them on. Then, still yawning, and absent-mindedly, as if I didn't know what I was doing, I reached up in back under the scarf and undid the bun. My hair fell down under the scarf, and I played around with my bobby pins, arranging them around the Coke glass, making designs, chewing my lips as if I were thinking about something else.

All this was totally unnecessary because he was still looking out the window. But you never know what kind of sideways vision people have. I shook my head as if I were too hot, or scratchy, wrinkled up my face and untied the scarf. When he looked back at me again I was all there with my naked face. The only thing missing was lipstick, which would have given me a few more years. Still, he saw the long dark hair, yellow eyes, oval face; and of course when I take all that stuff off, it's a real transformation. So naturally he looked surprised.

Since I didn't have lipstick to add some years, I got out my cigarettes and lit one real quick, just so he wouldn't get worried. He was staring at me, listening to the music at the same time, and he didn't say anything. When the record stopped he put on another, "Sentimental Journey." Then he came back, nodding his head in time to the music, "You like this stuff?"

"It's old," I said.

"Yeah," he said, still keeping time and staring at me. He had a lovely deep voice, I realized. I hadn't noticed it right away, but that's what good men's voices do to me, sort of sneak up on me. I love good voices!

He nodded toward the bar. "Harry hasn't changed this music since the war. When the old records wore out he kept getting new copies. He still gets them. This was a swinging establishment then. I think he's never gotten over it." I've never seen anyone stare so much, as if he didn't give a darn whether you cared he was staring or not. Those brown eyes just kept looking and looking, and it made me feel pretty strange.

"You want to take a walk?"

"Hm, hm," I mumbled quickly, a little scared.

"Where's your husband?" he finally asked.

I don't know what got into me, because the safest thing would have been to say, "Oh, around," or something like that. But instead I said, "I don't have a husband. I just wear the ring and everything because of people like that drunk."

He just nodded, "So you don't want to be picked up —okay."

If I *had* been married, I'd have been there to be picked up, but since I wasn't married, he understood perfectly. It made me dizzy, and he kept right on staring as if it didn't make a bit of difference whether I'd take a walk with him or not, or whether I was married or not.

"What's your birthday?" he suddenly asked.

"Oh, I'm not twenty-one yet . . ." I thought he wanted to know my age, so I left it wide open but young.

"What are you, seventeen? Eighteen?"

I shrugged, a little disturbed that he hadn't thought nineteen or twenty.

"I don't care," he said, "I didn't mean that anyway. What's your birth *day?*"

"March 7," I said, surprised.

"What time of day?"

I was surprised and had to think a minute before I told him.

He took out a little book from his shirt pocket and looked in it. "Pisces. With Gemini rising."

I think my jaw dropped. He didn't seem to be someone who'd be interested in astrology at all!

"I'm Scorpio," he said, "with Leo rising." Just as if it were an introduction! As if he'd given me his *name!*

"You're not eighteen yet," he frowned, still staring. "And you shouldn't smoke, you know. Pisces and Gemini . . . some combination! If you come out here again, and want to give me your year, I might like to fool around with your chart. Don't worry, not you—just your chart. Hold on, I want to spin another." He went to the juke box again.

I felt glued to my seat, the whole thing was so strange.

"This is my favorite," he said when he sat down again. "I usually play it last. Bet you've never heard it. Listen to this." He sang along as the record started, and he had a great singing voice, too.

It was "Lili Marlene," and of course I'd heard it.

"It's a German ditty, straight out of World War Two," he said. "Our guys picked it up and sang it all the time. This is the only bar in the world where you can really go back to the 40's, and nobody appreciates it except me. Me and the bird and Harry. And I'm not too sure about Harry. I'd sure like to know that bird's birthday. Harry's never been able to tell me. I think he's kind of out of it. Want another Coke? Or a shot? How about a brandy alexander? That's just about your speed."

He whipped the dollar off the table and went to the bar. "No cream," he called back. "How about cognac?"

He didn't even wait for my answer, but came back with two cognacs, his boots clicking on the floor in tune to "Lili Marlene." Those black boots were so wild on him! They just didn't go!

Outside it had started to rain in a thin drizzle, and then just as he sat down it really broke. The sky got very dark and sheets of water stormed against the window. Harry turned on the lights, and Scorpio—I didn't have any other name for him—looked terribly happy, as if the whole thing really suited him. As if he were in his element now in the dark bar with the rain and the cognac.

He took up his glass and clinked it with mine, "*Salut!* This is what they drank all over the ETO in World War Two."

He was the most fascinating character I'd ever met in my life! There's a word for him, the way he looked and talked, and made me feel. Magnetic. It was like he could draw a circle around us, pull everything in closer and closer. It wasn't just the rain and the strange feeling you'd naturally have in a far-off place like that with the blackness and storm all around. It was mainly *him*.

I didn't really mean to drink the cognac, but I was getting so pulled into the whole atmosphere that I automatically repeated, "Salut!" and drank. And choked. I'd never had cognac—or anything hard before—and I glanced at Harry the bartender to see if he'd noticed that I wasn't used to it.

Scorpio said, "Don't worry about Harry. You can come here anytime. He can hardly see. You don't have to worry about your age, either. I'm usually here anyway."

That made me feel very friendly! It sounded as if he'd be there to protect me. "Don't you go to school?" I asked, just dying to know his age.

His eyes got shielded and he shook his head.

"Where are you from?" I asked. The cognac had gone straight down, very warm, and then straight up to my head like a clear breeze, and I felt bold enough to ask questions.

But he wouldn't answer any of them. Not where he was from, or where he lived presently, or what he did, or his age—not even his name! Finally he looked as if he'd had enough of all my questioning, and he said, "Look, Pisces, I don't come out here for this. I don't answer any questions here. I don't even want to know your name. I don't need to know anybody's name. I don't know why you're here, and I'm not going to ask. If you want to say anything, go ahead. If not, it's not any of my business. Finish that and I'll get us another."

While Harry was pouring the drinks, he went up and said something to the bird who immediately went off again. "Buy war bonds! Buy war bonds! Buy war bonds!"

The other couple at the bar had left, and we were all alone. Scorpio, Harry, the bird, and me. The juke box played "Beer Barrel Polka," and he came back with the drinks, and I took another sip and got dizzy. I felt the whole room was somewhere up in the sky going round and round—like Dorothy's house in *The Wizard of Oz*. Then that stopped and I felt okay again, but very excited and talkative, and like I knew everything. I decided he was nineteen. I was *sure* he was nineteen! He just smiled. I decided his name was Heathcliff, and he raised his eyebrows. There was something definitely Heathcliffish about him. I said, "Okay, I'll just call you Scorpio."

He smiled. "Might as well say Leo. But how about something really fitting, since you know so much about me? Something like Dwight, Franklin, or why not Winston?"

I knew *nothing* about him! Also, I must have been getting drunk which is why it took me a minute to get it. Eisenhower, Roosevelt, and Churchill—the 1940's of course! Ordinarily I'm very quick on things like that. I smiled. "Oh no, not for you! You've got to be

Heathcliff. Or maybe Svengali? Rasputin?"

He looked impressed and his expression gave me confidence, so I leaned across the table, "Bet you'd never guess my father's name—Overbrook!"

He looked wary. "Don't worry," I said, "I'm not going to tell you my name, but his name really is Overbrook. And my mother's name is Wanda!" I drew it out long, "Waaanda. How about that?" Really, this all seemed so important at the time.

"Wanda," he mused, "Wanda the Witch and Raggedy Ann."

Well, this was the absolute end of the world! He couldn't have said anything better! What a bond between us. I felt I had known him for ever and ever and that we were twin souls destined for eternity together. He was Heathcliff and I was Cathy. I was really thinking stuff like that, I was getting so drunk without knowing it.

"You know the right witch!" I cried delightedly. "Not from *Sesame Street*, from *Raggedy Ann*."

"Shhh," he frowned, not wanting me to alert Harry at the bar to this particular conversation.

"And she really is a witch," I said, leaning way over.

"That old stuff's great," he said, far away again. "I love that old stuff. Remember all the sodas? They were always drinking sodas. Remember Snoopwiggy? I dug Snoopwiggy. Where did you get *Raggedy Ann* books, anyway?"

"She's a witch," I said, back on my own track. "My mother . . ."

"Oh, your mother's books," he nodded.

"And her name is Wanda," I repeated, because the whole thing was beginning to come together and make sense to me and I wondered why I hadn't seen it before. "She's not Wanda the Witch, she's a witch named Wanda!" To me that was absolutely brilliant.

"What's her birthday?" he asked.

I wasn't interested in that. I was interested in telling him my story. I was determined to tell him my story because he was so uninterested. He couldn't care less, and I wanted to show him what a witch she really was and make him care.

"She's not here," I said, finishing off my cognac. "She's skipped."

"What's her birthday?" His was really a one track mind. You couldn't move him.

"June," and I gave him the day but couldn't give him the time because I didn't know.

"Gemini, but wouldn't be Cancer rising if she's skipped. Is she very careless or very orderly?"

"Orderly." I couldn't help noticing that the idea of "skipping" hadn't impressed him. My mind was like a clear, sharp bell!

"Could be Virgo rising, they usually don't leave a mess."

"She washed the dishes before she left," I said. He was beginning to get me involved in this, too. I was curious. "And left a note."

He wouldn't commit himself. "Could be several things. Bring me out her year and time and I'll let you know. Where'd she go? Or don't you want to say? I don't really care—don't say." Maybe he was beginning to feel the drinks, too. After all, he'd had a few beers probably before I even saw him, plus mine and the cognac.

But I *had* to tell him, "She went to India."

This character was fantastic! Do you know all he did was nod and go for more cognac? As if everybody just toddled off to India!

Almost before he sat down again I said, "She left us and went to India. Left us all alone, my father and me." It sounded so sad I could have cried. "And my brother's gone, too. Sometimes I think the whole world is going, going, gone."

I stared down at my cognac glass with the hair falling over my face, and I felt like one of those lost, romantic, desolate women, except that something was missing. I remembered that it was a cigarette, and this time he lit it for me. I blew the smoke up sideways, like you're supposed to do in those deals, and looked off into space.

He seemed to take pity on me because he got very nice and sympathetic, and asked the questions that would let me tell my story. "What's she doing in India? Working?"

"No," I said. "Well, yes. Yes she is. She's resting and working."

"Go by boat?" he wasn't really interested though.

"No," I said miserably. "She flew."

He laughed, "On her broomstick?"

You see, he wasn't so drunk. *He* hadn't forgotten about Wanda the Witch, but I had.

"Oh, no," I recovered quickly, "Witches don't use broomsticks these days. They drop out by plane—on American Express."

That's when he got interested. I don't know if it was my tone, or what, but his whole expression changed. With a funny smile he leaned forward. "What?"

"They do! At least she did. She got fed up and left. She had this card like my father's you see, that she never used. And then she used it. She just freaked out on American Express."

His face lit up like a skyrocket and he started to

laugh. "That's what I thought you said, but I didn't believe it! Oh no! You don't mean it! You don't mean she really did it! Did she really do it?"

What a transformation! This eerie, serious guy—and all of a sudden he was ten years old. I was mad.

"She sure did, and I don't see what's so funny about it."

"Oh man, oh man, oh man!" He stamped a boot on the floor and even the bartender stared at him he was laughing so hard. "Oh, lord, I knew I came to Tottenville for something. Maybe this is it!"

Five

After that Scorpio seemed to regard me differently. I had the impression that he admired my mother more than any human being on the face of the earth, and that I was just basking in her reflected glory! It was a definite impression, but then I was drunk, and that has to be taken into consideration, too. Why did he admire her? What was so great about mother? I wanted to ask him, but could hardly get my tongue around answers to questions he was already asking me.

I didn't know what three cognacs had done to me until I needed to go to the ladies' room and couldn't. I mean I couldn't get up. Everything was swimming, and of course I wouldn't admit that for anything in the world. So I hung on and stared at my empty glass until it came into focus. Then I looked at the door to the street, and I do remember this distinctly because it was such an enormous effort; I stood up.

"I have to go. Good-bye."

He just waved! He didn't get up, take me out, or anything. "Roger! Hey, don't forget to bring the birth times, yours and Wanda's. Particularly Wanda's."

I guess he didn't have any idea how really stoned I was. I don't know how I looked, but I felt like that horrible old guy. I made a beeline for the door, and somehow got out. I had to stand there, holding on for a minute, and heard the music start again: "Pistol Packin' Mama." It wasn't raining so hard anymore, just drizzling. I took huge gulps of air as I maneuvered across the street. I knew I wasn't walking straight, and I had to go all the way down the hill. Then it was only a few feet to the train shed, and up in front of me stretched that long cement walk. The incline looked so steep, and then it looked flat, and then it went way up again. By this time I was admitting to myself what was the matter. I mean I was admitting I was drunk. I'd never been drunk before, naturally. In fact all I'd ever had to drink were tastes of beer and sips of my father's wine, which he insisted we try, because he's such a big wine expert. He thinks all children should grow up knowing good wines from bad ones, so they'll know how to order when they grow up. Also he thinks it's an aid to digestion. Oh, he has a big thing about wine.

Anyway, you can imagine how I felt on my first three cognacs. And I discovered something about being drunk. No matter how drunk you are, you'll never admit it to anyone but yourself. I stood there looking up the ramp, saying to myself, "I'm drunk and therefore I've got to act very, very not-drunk."

I waited until the ramp flattened out and started up. I was really walking uphill but it felt exactly like going down. The train was waiting there with two little figures in blue beside it. Then there was another one and I wondered why they'd have three conductors? I'd completely forgotten that my hair was down, and hadn't put on my scarf, so my hair was all wet.

The three conductors ran down the ramp towards me. I wasn't falling down or anything, so I wondered why. And then I got very elegant. This is difficult to describe, but I just know how drunks can get terribly elegant inside. So elegant that they can accept anything at all. Like the three conductors turning into one as they got near me, and there wasn't anything strange about it.

Guess who! Of course it had to be him. He had a big black umbrella under his arm, and he put it up over me even though the shed was overhead. He tucked my arm under his and we sort of scuttled up the ramp together. Honestly, I think my legs were bending. But I was very ladylike! I remember that we chatted, but I'm not too clear about what. Something about the weather, I think, and he was very cheery about everything always clearing up for everybody, the weather and everything. And my hair would dry out, and I said it didn't matter at all. I *liked* wet hair! He talked about Brooklyn, too, something about a garden because I remember pictures of flowers in my head. Lots of other stuff, too, that's just a blur. Then he put me in the back car—and I do remember this: he made lots of jokes going up and down the aisle. "How do you like our club car! Don't we have a lovely railroad!"

Somewhere around then I must have been out of it. I don't remember the train actually starting, just a general underneath movement that made me sick. I came to somewhere just before Old Town Road and had to go to the bathroom, and there wasn't any, and I was sick and dizzy all the way to St. George. It was very dark outside the windows and I thought it was rain. I didn't even know it was actually night until I left the train. The conductor waved goodbye, refused to take my ticket, which I only remembered to give him when we stopped, and said why didn't I hang on to it until next time. "The next time you want a ride in our club car."

At the ferryhouse I wished I were good and drunk or passed out again. I've never felt so ghastly in all my life. My head was going in and out like an expanding gong, my stomach kept gurgling and rising to my throat, and everything looked horrible. The ticket windows, the candy stands, the walls, the gate: it was all just grim, grim, grim! I kept swallowing while I waited for them to let down the gangway to the boat. And wouldn't you know, I didn't walk into a clean lovely compartment in the ladies room? It made me even sicker to be in it, and I had to throw up.

When I finally got out on deck it was black outside. It had stopped raining, the stars were out, the sky very clear, the lights in the city twinkling along with the boat lights all over the harbor. I stayed starboard, away from the Statue of Liberty, with my hands on the rail, and don't think I changed position once. I just let the wind blow and slap my face and whip my hair back while I kept opening my mouth like a frog, swallowing air.

Just before we pulled into Manhattan I had a horrible recollection. It was Sunday! My father's day off. He was going to be there when I got home—and I'd said *movies!*

I was too weak to make a plan, think up a good lie. All the way up in the subway I tried to think and couldn't. The subway stop is Eighty-sixth and Lexington, and I go way over near East End Avenue. It's always better to walk on Eighty-sixth Street because of the lights and stores. There's a crosstown bus, too, but I thought the walk would do me good. I couldn't tell you if anyone noticed my condition or not, I was so fuzzy. I saw a clock in a store that said a quarter of twelve—and I panicked. Then I looked closer and saw it was really only 9 P.M.

But that was still too late! A movie only takes a couple of hours, and I'd been gone all day. My stomach and head were still going round, and all I wanted to do was dive into bed, and not think. Outside our house I stopped for a while, trying to force myself to think, and then I went just—blah. So what, blah! I pulled myself up the few steps by the iron railing, went to the hall and opened our front door.

Now, here's one of those things that happen all the time, except that they never happen when you want them to. Sometimes they do, but you can never count on it. Maybe you have to be "blah" like I was to run into a thing like this, I don't know.

My father was *asleep* on the living-room couch with the theater section of the *Times* half over his face and the rest of the paper all over him like a blanket except for his skinny toes, which were sticking out. The paper blew up and down as he breathed. Well! I held my breath and tiptoed past him all the way back to my room. I got undressed and into my nightgown and sat on the side of the bed because I was dizzy. I couldn't get sick and throw up again! We only have one bathroom, and the flush is very loud, and I knew he'd hear me. He had probably fallen asleep an hour or so ago, and if I knew his habits he was good until around eleven thirty when he'd wake up again.

I got very hot all of a sudden like I was burning up. I *had* to have water, even though the thought of more liquid churning around made me sick. But I was actually sweating, so I went out to the kitchen sink and held a glass under the faucet that always has a light drip. I didn't dare turn on the water. I just waited while the drops fell, plink-plink-plink. It took ages and ages to get even half a glass, which I took back to my room. And the drip is on the hot water side so it was very warm and horrible.

My room is a typical, nice, New York girl's room. Or maybe you'd say a nice girl's New York room. It's small and thoroughly decorated. I had recently fallen in love with purple, so I had a purple Indian print bedspread and curtains, a shaggy purple rug, a bowl of huge purple paper flowers, even purple candles and some purple incense Dick had given me. I have a tall bookcase, a radio on a shelf over my bed, a built-in desk cupboard combination, and some old kiddie animals on my bed. I keep lots of my clothes in pull-out drawers built in under the bed, because my closet is so small. And there were my old Raggedy Ann and Raggedy Andy, sitting up next to their own books in the bookcase, with their legs falling down from the shelf. They were pretty faded, smiling characters.

Like everyone else I know I have very colorful posters on the wall over my bed. Two of them are Op Art posters with crazy circles and squares that look like one thing and then another depending on how you look at them. After drinking the warm water I fell back on my bed sort of panting, and those posters seemed to just lean over on me. I didn't mean to look at them, but one glance and it was all over. The bed started spinning, I reared up and grabbed onto the side, trying not to throw up, swallowing, swallowing . . .

I had to stay in that position half the night! I didn't dare lie down. When I finally heard my father get up an hour later, I ducked under the covers in a ball and tried to hold the position. I knew he was going to come take a look. I could feel him trying to decide whether to wake me up and ask where I'd been. I did wish he'd hurry up about it. I was in that ball, with my knees way up, holding my breath. Not because I didn't want him to hear me breathe; after all that's sort of reassuring. I just couldn't let my breath out because if I did I'd throw up. *Finally* he closed the door and went away. I'd have locked it then, except that we don't have locks because of the thing about privacy. We've never needed locks, at least not until then.

I had to sit upright until two or three in the morning when my stomach stopped churning. All during this time I had crazy visions. You'd have to go through this to know what I mean, and I'm not suggesting that it's absolutely necessary to know. In fact I'd be just delighted not to know! It's that early-morning, in-between, half-drunk-but-not-quite, sick, woozy, misty world . . .

I began to think the Raggedys were real and that we were all talking together silently, including Scorpio out there in Tottenville. I couldn't remember what kind of a witch Wanda was, good or bad, and thought I should look in the books, but I couldn't move. And the conductor came into this, and the bird, and then I thought I was forty years old, seeing my whole life pass by. And then I imagined I was Cathy with Heath-cliff out on the moors, and superimposed the moors on all those weeds in Tottenville. And I imagined my father getting very drunk and coming after me like that horrible brother of hers. I mean Hindley Earnshaw.

All this on a few cognacs! It went round and round, but mostly that beautiful Scorpio with Leo rising whose name I didn't know and probably wasn't ever going to know. Then, somewhere along the way, I guess I just toppled over and konked out.

Six

Once Dick and I went on a family summer vacation up in Vermont. Daddy rented a car and we all drove around, staying one place for a night, another for longer, just depending on how we liked it. We really covered the state of Vermont, which is a beautiful, really gorgeous place. Well, just toward the end of our trip we found an old farmhouse on a side road with a sign saying they took in boarders. We went in for the night and then stayed three days, until the end of our vacation. They had great food, like five courses, including eggs and pancakes for breakfast, and wonderful old rooms with chamber pots and spider webs and creaky chairs and stringy rugs and real damp, clammy old quilts that had been mended a hundred times on top of lumpy old mattresses. All this, including the food, only cost $3.50 a day for each person! I remember that because it made such a big impression on my father.

We took over the whole second floor, all three bedrooms, and the farm family lived downstairs all together in one big room just off the kitchen. I peeked into that room once and it looked like a storage. It was so stuffed with old furniture and junk and old clothes and rags, that you could hardly see the beds. Four kids plus two adults slept in there at night, and it reminded me of a litter. You know, it was just the

sort of place you'd expect to find ten puppies or something. I guess they put all their best junk upstairs for
the boarders, and at first I felt sort of sorry for them.
But by the end of the second day I didn't feel sorry at
all.

There were three boys and one girl, from about
fifteen down to eleven, and they looked like the mean-
est, angriest bunch of kids I'd ever seen. After I saw
more of the mother and father I could see where they
got it. That man was so mean he reminded me of
Captain Bligh, except he wasn't as smart. He was
dumb, and mean. The mother wasn't so dumb, but she
had these hard little black eyes that kept following
the kids whatever they did. They could hardly breathe
without her noticing. They had to stand in the kitch-
en and peel potatoes and help with the washing and
go out and chop wood. I never saw them outside
playing or even getting air or anything like that. They
did make maple syrup in the early, snowy spring, so
maybe the kids got some fresh air then. Although it's
possible they just stood inside and stirred or whatever it is you do with maple syrup. They were very
pale and pasty-looking.

We, of course, were outside all the time, taking long,
gorgeous hikes. That house was really in one of the
prettiest settings I've ever seen. Then we'd go back for
an enormous dinner, and everyone ate together at a
large table. In absolute silence! That is, my parents
talked to Captain and Mrs. Bligh as much as they
could, which wasn't much, and all the kids just ate.
If anybody did the wrong thing, like grabbing the
butter, the Captain would reach out his huge hairy
hand and go *whap!* And the mother's eyes would get
even harder and you'd figure next she was going to
torture them or something.

Dick and I felt so out of place that we didn't talk

either. We were as silent as they were. Our dinner times were very different, you see, particularly on weekends when my father was home. We talked about books, music, plays, politics, elections, poverty, foreign affairs and the state of the world.

All the MLU's seem to be like that. They keep feeding the kids with lots of facts that are supposed to lead to questions so we can grow up to ask more questions and be more understanding. All my friends had the same experience. Sometimes we'd get so tired of it we'd want to turn the whole thing off. I think that's when some of the kids go and smoke grass. But then, the parents understand that, too, how tired you are. So they'll suddenly come down to something real fun and old-fashioned, like going to the park to fly a kite or sledding. It's a relief, but it's also kind of a mean trap. For a little while everything seems so normal, and then, before you know it, you're back in the world's problems again. Sometimes I used to wish they wouldn't say anything at all, and just let us find out!

But now that we were actually in that sort of situation, it didn't look too great, either. How could these kids ever learn anything? Naturally we figured such mean, dumb kids, having such mean, dumb parents, were automatically going to turn into monsters and wind up in the same kind of farmhouse whapping *their* kids. Imagine our surprise on the last day when we discovered that one boy wanted to be an electrician, another wanted to be a lawyer, another was already learning TV repair, and the girl was going to study nursing.

Since we were leaving I guess they figured it was safe to talk to us. My father was paying the bill in the kitchen and the kids stood around the living room looking at us, and that's when all this came out. Well, that family had so little communication that I couldn't figure it out. How did they know what they wanted to be so early? Dick and I didn't have the slightest idea yet!

"Did you take aptitude tests in schools?" I asked one boy.

"Naw."

"Do you like to help sick people?" I asked the girl.

She stared at me as if *I* were dumb or crazy. "I dunno—got to do something . . ."

Then the kid who wanted to be a lawyer got very impatient, I think he was a lot brighter than the others. He said, "Oh, you don't understand! People who live like this up here—we've got to get *out!*"

And honest to goodness I had the impression we were living on different planets! All the way down to Connecticut in the car I couldn't get over it. I mean, you'd just naturally assume that kids like that would want to be dropouts, delinquents, hippies! And instead, their idea of getting *out* was to become an electrician, lawyer, nurse!

My father, who hadn't even heard that conversation, still thought the whole thing had been a great experience for us. "Now you can see the way to raise kids! That's the way to raise kids, Wanda!" He was being funny, you know. He was very amused. "The trouble with you kids is that we're not strict enough with you!"

He said it exactly as if it were our fault.

"I remember my grandfather . . ."

And off he went into the same old story about how his father had told him that *his* father used to walk through the house at precisely 9 P.M. each night, carrying with him his old-fashioned alarm clock which he had set for some horrible hour in the morning. It didn't matter if anyone had company or not. The old man got rid of everybody by waving the clock right in front of them. Every time my father tells this story he

chuckles and threatens to do it to us, instead of quietly disappearing into his bedroom so we can have our
privacy. Well, that's idiotic! Nobody does that, and of
course he'd never do it. My parents are very good
about things like that.

The reason I went into these stories is because of
what happened next. It involves understanding, and
you've got to have the two pictures next to each
other to see it. I woke up with this ghastly hangover,
and of course I didn't feel like going to school. There
were three days left until summer vacation. So I lay
there in bed with my head aching and wondered how
to get out of it. In other words, what would be the
best approach with my father.

Honestly, with these MLU's you've got to be a mas-
ter shrink! You've got to keep one step ahead of them
all the time, figure out all the angles, "pre-think" them,
and then make a choice for them. It can be very tiring
and I didn't feel up to it. With that mean old farmer
I wouldn't have had to think at all. I hate to think
what he would have done to me. As a matter of fact I
did think of him the minute I woke up facing all these
decisions. I wondered if it wouldn't be sort of relaxing
to have a monster like that around. It'd all be over in
a minute. On the other hand, I don't go begging for
trouble.

Ordinarily it would only have taken a second to
dream up a good lie. But the situation had changed,
you see. Mother wasn't there! And because of that, I
had an uncomfortable feeling that my father might
not react in his usual way. He might not believe me, or
he might get tough because he wouldn't know what to
do without my mother, and so forth. It was a dilem-
ma. I chewed on it, back and forth, until all of a sudden I had it. It was ridiculously simple! The answer
had been there all the time.

The very best thing I could say was that I was upset, had gone out to be alone, had therefore lied about the movies, had gotten drunk and had a hangover!

It was so obvious! Naturally I'd be upset and do all these things, and naturally he would be understanding. I was almost sorry he hadn't seen me last night, after all, because he would have been even sorrier, and even more understanding about my condition.

There was only one thing. I was determined *nobody* was going to know about Tottenville. So I thought I'd say that I was at a girl's house, we found some bottles and so forth. It was beautiful!

Seven

I was sitting up in bed, feeling weak, sick, and terribly thirsty, when I heard the telephone ring and my father go to answer it. I went to the bathroom, had three fast glasses of water while he was talking, and then he called me. I trailed out to the front room in my nightgown, and it turned out to be my brother Dick calling from California. He wanted to know if he should come home.

"Are you okay?" he asked.

He sounded a little upset, so I gathered my father had told him about mother.

"Sure, I'm okay. Where are you?" I asked.

"In a telephone booth."

Dick always answers things that way, telling you what you don't want to know.

"Do you think I should come home?" he said. "Are you going to be all right?"

I was amazed at all this consideration! I sat down on the couch because my head was pounding, and watched my father go out into the front hall. He always sneaks out there in his shorts and tee shirt which he wears to sleep in instead of pajamas to get the milk, paper, and mail.

"Sure, I'm going to be okay, I'm just fine."

"Have you heard from mother yet?"

"Just a short note." Ordinarily I like to talk to Dick. Now that we're both older, we don't compete any more. But right now my head was pounding so badly I didn't want to talk to anyone.

"Listen, what got into her anyway? Was it me? I mean, splitting from school? Dad wouldn't say. He's like a clam. Or was it him? Did he do something? Come on Jane, are you there?"

"Yes, I'm here. And it wasn't you particularly. Or, I don't know, maybe it was. That post card from the beach. But it could have been Daddy, too, going to Albany."

"What'd he go to Albany for?"

"Oh, it was one of those deals, and he didn't call in time, and then your post card came the same morning. I guess it was everybody. A whole bunch of last straws at the same time. Me, too."

"What did you do?"

Naturally he would suddenly sound like the big older brother! I had a weird feeling, in spite of Dick's run-away style, that if I told him the truth—that *I* had tried to run away—he would come home and crack down on me and it might be horrible. So I lied. "Oh I didn't do much of anything. It wasn't important. She just found some cigarettes in my room."

Long ago I discovered that lying on a truthful basis almost always works. Nobody can catch you up. This was a little mean of me, however, because it didn't make mother look too great.

"Cigarettes! *That's* all that set her off? That's incredible!" There was a pause and then he said, "Listen, Jane, she knew I'd already split. What difference would it make to her whether I was at the college or on the beach? And Dad's been going off like that for years. She knows he doesn't always call to let her know in advance. Sometimes he can't. And now you're telling me she found *cigarettes* and flipped? Look, is she really all right? Or is she having some sort of a breakdown? Is she *really* in India or isn't Dad telling me the truth?"

I got angry at this implication that she might actually be in a mental hospital. "I don't see what you're so amazed about! *You* dropped out! Why does she have to crack up just to drop out?"

"Because mothers don't do those things! What's the matter with you anyway? You know it isn't normal. It just isn't done!"

"Well, she did it," said I, and it sounded strange even to me. And vaguely I wondered how come I was suddenly defending her?

"And *India?*" he insisted. "Mothers don't just disappear to India—to *ashrams?* Come on, Jane, that's kid stuff. That's for hippies."

"Why does she have to be a kid?" I asked. "She's been interested in that stuff longer than the kids. I guess she just went there because she's always wanted to go there."

"But you just don't go any old place you want to go . . ." His voice trailed away, and I could almost hear him thinking it was exactly what he had done. "At least mothers don't," he added weakly, and I could hear him take a deep breath way out there in California.

I tried to change the subject. "Is it sunny out there? What beach are you on? Listen, maybe I could come out and go surfing with you. What time is it out there, anyway?"

There was a long, long pause. I tried to visualize Dick in his swim trunks, all tanned, standing in a telephone booth on the sand under the hot sun, near the crashing waves. He's a good-looking boy. Tall, with brown hair, and the same yellow eyes as me. He looks great with a tan. Girls like him.

"It's five o'clock in the morning," he said, giving me a slight shock.

"How long is your hair now?" I asked, when he didn't answer any of my other questions.

There was another long pause, and then, heaven knows why, he gave me the straight dope. "I just called for some money. Thought I might get a bus back home. I've sort of had it out here. In fact it's a mess. The guys I'm staying with are splitting—arguments all the time. Some of them are going to Acapulco and I don't want to hitch on."

"Well?"

"Well—so tell Dad to send me some bread."

"Why don't you ask him?"

"I already did."

"And?"

"He's cagey. Won't say yes or no. I don't know what's the matter with him, either. He's sent me money before in a jam."

"Yes, but that was just for pot," I said meanly, because I was upset again. Now I understood all this so-called concern. For a minute I'd thought he was going to act like an old-fashioned big brother, and didn't realize I liked the idea, until I found out it wasn't true. "What did you ask him for this time? How much?"

"Just bus fare," he kind of begged.

He was really pleading with me to intervene, and I began to feel powerful, like I guess women do when men have to come to them for things. It was a strange feeling, nasty and good at the same time. I was trying to figure out if I even *wanted* him back home, when my father came back in. He'd been out there in the hall an awfully long time.

He shut the door slowly behind him as he looked down at the floor. Everything about him, even his legs, looked whiter than usual. My father has that really pale skin where every mole and every hair and every blemish shows up, the type that can't take the sun for even three minutes. So for me to notice this sudden bloodlessness of his shows how truly white he was at that moment. Actually, he wasn't looking at the floor. He was staring at some mail in his hand which was white, too, and sort of blended in with him, which was why I hadn't noticed it right away.

He looked at me, saw that I was still on the phone, and his neck veins bulged red. His knees and elbows got pink like they always do when he's angry. He grabbed the receiver out of my hand so fast that I jumped.

"Next time you call here, Dick, you put your own nickels in!" he shouted out to California. "I'm not accepting any more collect calls. Clear?"

I gaped at him.

Two seconds later he said, "I don't give a damn what your problem is. Get back on your own steam if you want to come back. Figure it out! You're not getting any more free excursions from this end." Wham! Bam! He hung up, just like that.

I couldn't believe my ears. He'd never talked to Dick so toughly before. Then it dawned on me what must be dangling from his hand. The American Express bill had arrived! I tried to read it upside down, but all I could see was lots of numbers that looked dreadfully long and like over $1000. He crumpled it up and barked at me, "Don't you accept any more collect calls from your brother under *any* circumstances. Or from *anyone!*"

"She isn't going to call all the way from India," I protested vaguely. Then I was so curious I just had to ask, "Was it really over $1000?"

It was the wrong thing to say. He looked even grimmer than old Captain Bligh. I froze, thinking he might whap me. But instead he stomped off to his bedroom, obviously trying to keep his temper under control.

My head was going thump-zing, zing-thump, and my stomach felt awful. I was sorry he'd hung up on Dick so abruptly, and I started worrying. It hit me all of a sudden. I looked around and thought of poor Dick out there, stranded, unable to come back. Maybe he was thinking about this room. Maybe he was visualizing being here. After all, even if it wasn't a house, it was our home. We'd grown up here, mother had put a lot of effort into it. All the early American antique furniture, the old prints and oils on the walls, the faded but good old Chinese rugs, the plants making a second garden at the front windows—they looked awfully dusty and drooping, I noticed.

For some reason I thought of birthday candles. I saw lots of birthday candles on lots of birthday cakes, and remembered all sorts of different birthday parties mother had given for us.

Maybe it was just the hangover, but my throat tightened and I felt so rotten I almost began to cry. Dick might actually be homesick, and I didn't even know where to call him back! And then I finally realized *I* was homesick, too!

"Where were you last night?" my father confronted me, coming out of his room all dressed. He still looked angry, and I knew something had changed. He wasn't going to be understanding this time. I couldn't possibly say I'd been drunk.

"I just went over to a friend's house," I lied quickly.

"Without calling me!"

Father's eyes are light blue and can be very piercing when he is really paying attention to something. Otherwise they're sort of pale and mild, like an old baby quilt. They were flashing now, and picking up the sharp blue of his striped tie. It was his imported English one, and he was wearing his Brooks Brothers suit, so I knew he must have somewhere crucial to go. His wardrobe is very scant. He has this one great suit and otherwise doesn't seem to care what he wears. Usually, with that suit on, you couldn't talk to him about anything. He'd be thinking about his appointment, mentally rehearsing the whole thing. This was the first time he'd *ever* talked to me while he was wearing that suit, and it made me very uneasy.

"I—forgot," I said lamely.

"Well you're not to forget again! In fact, you're not to go *anyplace* at night. I want you home, here, by five o'clock each day. In fact, if you go anyplace after school that'll keep you out until five o'clock, I want to know about it. I want to know where you are at all times!"

He sat down on the Windsor chair to tie his shoelaces, and I stared at him. He reminded me of that television announcer who comes on at night and asks in this sepulchral voice, *"Do you know where your children are?"*

He looked at his watch and frowned at me, "Why aren't you getting ready for school?"

I swallowed and ran my toe over a blue butterfly on the Chinese rug. "I don't feel well today. Not well enough to go to school. I feel sick."

That was the truth! But he suddenly came over to the couch, grabbed my chin, and peered into my eyes. He was looking for telltale red, you know, signs of grass. "Are you telling me the truth?"

"Yes, I *am*," I said, big-eyed and innocent, and praying that my breath was all right.

I guess he believed me, because he didn't say anything more, and a few minutes later he left. I watched him go out the front door in that Brooks Brothers suit, and for a second it looked pathetic. I felt sorry for him! *Why?* But my head was pounding so hard I didn't have room for such a brand new feeling.

Eight

The drumming in my head fought with pictures of Scorpio that blinked on and off like a series of slides. And I kept seeing that black bird. What I wanted to do was go back to Tottenville immediately, so Scorpio wouldn't forget me. I guess I was already halfway in love with him; at the very least totally fascinated with him. But it was even more than that.

I had a deep feeling that he was an important part of my experience during mother's absence. That he was connected with it, somehow, that he just *had to be*. Inevitability. Something like that. And it gave me a funny sense of security about him. This was really peculiar, but the very strangeness of him, the mystery surrounding him, the flavor of adventure, was the only *secure* thing I felt. It was really crazy to feel this flooding of security from the unknown. I wonder if Columbus could have felt like that? Or the guys on Apollo 11?

My home at that time seemed completely strange, and the only real place was Tottenville. I desperately wanted to go back. But my father had been so peculiar, that for the first time I was afraid. What would happen if he came home and didn't find me—after his lecture? I thought about calling the bar and leaving a message, but it seemed an awfully forward thing to do. I didn't even know what Harry the bartender called Scorpio. And what could I say? "I want to leave a message for the fellow in the black boots?" It sounded dreadful! Scorpio wasn't the type to appreciate girls leaving messages for him in a bar where he wanted to be anonymous. He might never go back there again! Then it occurred to me that I didn't even know the name of the bar! I was so hung over that my head wasn't working properly over any of this. So I tried to let it go and not think about it.

I sat on the couch after my father left, and noticed that the house needed cleaning. But when I stood up my stomach felt so awful that I sat down again. Now I know that it takes six to eight hours to get rid of a hangover and all you can do is live through it. But I didn't know this then, so I made myself even more uncomfortable by fighting it all the way.

I wished we had a dog or something to keep me company. Spot, our little goldfish, was long gone. I missed him—her—whatever Spot was. It was so silent, too. Not a sound in the apartment, and only a few cars going past outside. It wasn't that comfortable silence of knowing something was going to happen later on, so you could really appreciate it. I ran my toe over the blue butterfly again, wishing it were alive. Even going back to my childish game of pretending it was a fairy-tale friend. Ridiculous!

Everything seemed so sour. Just one big wasteland, including the ghastly taste in my mouth. It reminded me of Prufrock measuring his life out with coffee spoons. I couldn't help thinking "cognac spoons," but it didn't matter. I felt I finally understood the whole thing. It dawned on me suddenly that all teen-agers have *hope*—and there isn't any. And Prufrock knew it. Doleful things like that came to me, as if I were already ninety-six and on my way out.

In fact every bleak poem or story, author or composer that I'd ever read or heard seemed to move in on me all at once. Things I didn't even know I knew! As if some nerve channel had opened up. It felt as if a needle were playing a stereo groove in my brain that had formerly been asleep. Phrases came back, lines, everything. Kafka, Mahler, Poe, things from the Brothers Grimm—and what a name for them! Even, in its truly pathetic and terrible sense, "Who Killed Cock Robin?" Have you ever thought what a universal tragedy that little nursery rhyme is? I mean, you could connect it with anything—Vietnam, Martin Luther King, yourself, anything!

All these dour thoughts came, practically entombing me. Not silly monster movies or anything like that. This was the real thing with no Godzillas at all. And along with it I had a vision of acres and acres of lonely people all over the world in all the cities, sitting alone in their squalid little rooms, no sound, no company, no friends, no relatives. *Loneliness.*

I'd never known that word before, really. In me, or in what it meant. It started with that ashy wasteland in my mouth which was real, and not one of those mouthwash commercials with people skiing through my teeth. And it opened up to include *everything,* and it was horrible.

So I started really missing my mother. Naturally! Who wouldn't, at a time like that? I'm not making excuses for missing her, though. If I made any excuses, it would be for not missing her before. But who's to say I hadn't? I hadn't felt as if I missed her, but then I'd been sort of numb. I was so surprised, shocked, and upset about it—and baffled—that maybe there wasn't room for missing. Or maybe I hadn't let the feeling in. But now it overcame me.

You know those old-fashioned novels where maidens are "overcome" by love or tragedy and they proceed to faint? Well, you can be overcome by other things as well and not faint. You can just *feel*. Things such as missing your mother. Much as I hate to say this, it's true. It's been said by other people for thousands of years but it's still true. Excuse me, but there's nothing like your own mother and, in a way, there never can be.

I remembered when I was little and had fevers and she used to put her cool hand on my forehead. It was firm and gentle, and as well as enjoying the coolness, I remembered the total protection I felt from that, like Linus' blanket. It made me feel better right away. Well, in the midst of this terrible hangover, sicker than I'd ever felt with tonsillitis, I ached for my mother's hand on my forehead. Maybe it sounds silly, but I knew that if she'd been there I'd have relaxed, the demons would have flown, and things would just have taken their course.

You never miss the sunshine until the sun is gone . . .

That old saying came to me just then. How can such corny things sometimes be so true? It frightened me, and I didn't know why, until I remembered where I'd heard it. My mother had said it one night. She and my father and Mary's parents were sitting around until the wee hours discussing the possibilities for a popular television series. My father and Mary's father had an idea for a show, and they were talking about the essence of "popular corn." My mother had mentioned that, saying that her mother had told it to her.

And that frightened me even more. Could mother

have been thinking, or even *planning,* to be the "missing sunshine" way back then? That had been over a year ago, and the idea that she might have planned this terrified me.

What if she didn't come back?

But that was idiotic. She hadn't died. She had to come back.

But suppose she had "died to the world?"

Nonsense, I kept telling myself. As Dick said, women with children just didn't do that sort of thing! They didn't abandon their children and split to a nunnery. Properly speaking, there are no such things as nunneries. They are supposed to be called monasteries, even if they are for women. Anyway, mothers just didn't prance off to ashrams and stay there forever.

But suppose she did! Suppose she didn't consider it abandoning her children. Maybe she didn't regard us, at sixteen and eighteen, as children! That remark about Indian girls was very suspicious.

Suppose there was some weird guru over there telling her her job in life was finished, and sucking her into the fold. In some Hindu countries, and Buddhist as well, men and women get married, bring up their children, go through all the natural cycles, and then polish it all off with what is to them the last natural cycle of their old age. Contemplation, study, perhaps even staying in a monastery until they die. And the whole thing is perfectly acceptable to everyone. I'd heard mother talk about it. Oh, lord! She *had* talked about it!

"But she isn't old enough to throw away her life like that."

"Maybe she doesn't consider it throwing her life away," said the devil's—or maybe the angel's—advocate inside me. By this time I was in a real conversation with myself. "Maybe to her she *is* old. How do you know how old she feels after bringing up two kids and working for years?"

"But she's so young."

"And look how young she was when she started reading all that stuff. She's been reading it as long as I remember. Maybe in terms like that she's ancient."

"Well, no matter how ancient she may be that way, she's still under forty in this world, and she's got a family. She can't just walk out on her family!" One side of me said.

"Why not?" stated the other Jane flatly. "Her family's always walking out on her."

Boiiing! It was just as if a huge gong had gone off in the room, leaving a terrific reverberation between mother and us. Why, did she want to be free too? *Like us?* Did she feel like we did? Young and old at the same time? Ancient and infant and everything in between?

I was feeling like the *Three Faces of Eve,* and this third Jane, Spectator Jane, sat sort of squashed in the middle of that fantastic reverberation, struggling with this new concept of mother as person, not mother.

I want to make this very clear. The shock came because I'd always *thought* I thought of mother as a person. All children of MLU's do. They're brought up that way. But I suddenly saw that my idea of "person" was in the habits, way of moving, voice, looks, interests, wants. And over all that the idea of *mother* still loomed. All-pervasive, connected to me, really there *for* me. The force of thinking of her as a person there for herself, with not only wants but separate needs, was devastating. I felt completely cut off from her; that large part that had always been there for itself and not there for me at all.

"Yes," one Jane offered a little wickedly. "Remem-

ber this person reading to you from *The Prophet?*"
There was a passage she was particularly fond of,
which had to do with children not really belonging to
their parents, but being free and beautiful spirits who
are in their parents' care for just a little while.

"Yes," said the other Jane, remembering reluctantly.

"Well, if the children are free spirits—separate persons—then aren't the parents, too?"

Spectator Jane squirmed. "Somebody should have
spelled that out so we'd all be quite clear . . ."

But Western-oriented Jane rebelled. "It doesn't
make any difference! She's a Western mother, not an
Eastern one! We live in this culture, not that. An
American woman *can't* feel free-person first and
bound-mother second. She's got to be a mother-person,
not a person-mother!"

I, Spectator Jane in the middle, couldn't stand any
more of this. "Oh," I groaned aloud, and the words
seemed to push up from the bottom of a deep well,
"Oh, if *only* she'd just gone off to Miami!"

And I stared around the room, bug-eyed. If she'd
gone to Miami, everything would have seemed natural.
Exhaustion, plus anger, flipping out to a plush hotel
and spending lots of money. Why I, left at home,
would have a good time with that. I could have felt
superior, smug, knowing she'd be back.

There was something terrible here! Why would I
understand it better if she'd done something as commercial and vulgar as that? It even occurred to me that
we'd all understand it better if she'd gone off to have
an *affair!*

I can't tell you how awful all these thoughts were.
Weren't we supposed to be a real MLU family? Where
was all that understanding? Dick and I were supposed
to be so independent. Why then did I, at least, feel so
dependent?

"And on what?" the voices started again. "Dependent on what?"

"Mother, I guess, her presence."

"What is her presence?"

"I don't know! The glue, maybe?"

"What glue? For what?"

"I don't know! To *be* here! To hold things together. So we'll be free to leave when it's time."

"Aren't we free anyway? We're always leaving, or thinking about leaving. Dick's left!"

"Yes, but he had something to leave *from!* She was here. Oh, I don't know! Maybe she's got to be here to push us out."

"Are you telling me that a mother's job is to stick around and raise her kids in order to push them out? That's horrible!"

"I know. I may never get married."

"But it's horrible, horrible," the other Jane kept repeating.

"Why can't we all just be friends with mother?"

"We're supposed to be, but if we really were, I suppose we'd understand it better."

"Could you possibly be jealous?" asked one Jane very sneakily.

And with that thought ringing in my head I completely collapsed.

Little Jane in the middle whispered to herself, "But she did say she didn't know how long she'd stay, which must mean that she will be back someday."

I couldn't stand it any more! This was the way people landed in institutions! I had to see someone, talk to someone, have a human contact. I *had* to see Scorpio!

I leaped up from the couch with all these thoughts making a crossfire in my head over the drum beat of the hangover, and a solution darted in from nowhere.

I couldn't call the bar to leave an ordinary message, but I could call to leave Wanda's birth date.

Eureka! I knew Scorpio would love that. He wouldn't mind being called to the phone for a witch's horoscope. But first, I had to have her birth date. I knew the day, of course, but I didn't know the precise time or the year. Mother had always played a little joke with us about that. She'd say, "Oh, I'm over twenty-one!" Or, "Under ninety-two!" I figured she had to be around thirty-eight or forty, and I remembered seeing a card that could have been a birth announcement in one of the photograph albums.

We have an awful lot of photograph albums in this family, and we're the only people I know who never have loose snapshots lying around in shoe boxes. The reason is we have so little closet space. Fortunately mother is a filing fiend, and the albums are arranged in neat chronological order on the bottom shelf of our bookcase. But when I dashed out to the hall to look for her baby album, I saw it wasn't there. This series began with Dick and me. Whereupon I went into mother and daddy's room and looked in their small bookcase.

There were mother's books that I'd always seen there, Karma Yoga, The Bhagavad-Gita, the Bible, the Koran, one on Zen Buddhism, and an awful lot I hadn't seen before and didn't recognize. *The Way of Life, Commentaries on Living, Letters from the Scattered Brotherhood,* and *Seven Years in Tibet!* That one petrified me. I hadn't known she'd been picking up all this; they all looked new. The only reassuring things in the bookcase were her anthology of British poetry, and a couple of mysteries that I knew she read to try and put herself to sleep on the nights when my father was off on one of the projects.

Down on the bottom shelf were mother's and father's albums. I took them out, having a hard time ungluing my eyes from *Seven Years in Tibet*. Before I got too nervous over that, I shook out the albums hoping the birth announcement would fall out, and I wouldn't have to search for it. Lots of things fell out! Crumbling leaves, pressed flowers, duplicate photos, large graduation pictures, a piece of material, letters. And there it was.

In a blue-bordered envelope! They must have expected a boy! Did that explain anything, I wondered? The little card inside had a tiny blue silk bow attached to the top, and it was not handwritten. It was very elegantly printed in small, delicate type. Her name was at the top, with the date, time, and year below, and then my grandparents' names beneath. Her time of birth was 8:15 P.M.

I dashed out to the telephone with the card, picked up the receiver, and had already dialed 411, staring all the time at the card, when it struck me suddenly. She was *over* forty!

She'd crossed the border! Maybe she did want the next twenty or thirty years all for herself! But before I had time to panic again, the operator came on.

"May I help you?" It was such a relief to hear another voice besides my own!

I stumbled a little, asking if she could help me find a bar in Staten Island.

"You'll have to dial 555-1212."

I did, and asked the next operator, "I wonder if you could help me find a bar in Tottenville? I don't have the name of the bar, but it's at the top of the hill up from the railroad station."

"That's Tottenville, New York?"

"Yes—uh—Staten Island."

"What is the name of the bar?"

"I said I don't have the name."

"Well, what is the name of the street, please?"

"I don't know the street, but it's the next one up from the Tottenville station—"

She cut me off, "I'm sorry, miss, but without a name or location, I won't be able to help you. I'm not familiar with Staten Island and I don't know where the station is."

"Isn't there *anybody* there from Staten Island?" I begged.

"I'm sorry, miss. Without a name and location I can't help you." She hung up.

I left everything just as it was, album litter on the floor in the other room, albums strewn about in the hall, dusty plants, my father's slippers under the chair; I dressed in the prettiest, sexiest dress I had, pulled on my slob outfit of raincoat and scarf, and tore out . . . to find Tottenville again.

Nine

I was so frantic for human contact that I almost hoped my Santa Claus conductor would be on the train again. Instead there were two very young conductors who were entirely different, just as the day was different. It was bright and sunshiny with a sky so blue it almost hurt one's eyes. The lawns and trees were apple green, and there were sharp shadows everywhere. It was a perfect day for photographers, not for someone like me, desperately wanting Tottenville.

One of the conductors, who wore his cap at a rakish angle, was trying to impress a young girl with his charm. He sat down beside her, and really attacked the whole problem with zest. That's the sort of day it was. I watched them from under my scarf and glasses, huddling next to the window again. I could feel the edge of mother's birth announcement card in my raincoat pocket. Oh, if that wasn't a strange experience; riding that train on a day like that and carrying along a 1928 birth announcement. WANDA ROWENA GLAD WESTERLEY. The name jolted out of me with each jerk of the train. It's a terrible name, I said to myself.

Have you even been out on a bright, busy day like that, and yet been completely alone and in silence? All the sounds seemed to come from a great distance, and what I really heard was only in my own head. It went on all the way to Tottenville. I might as well explain that name of hers, which really was her real maiden name.

"Wanda" she said, came from who-knew-where? My Grandma Westerley would never discuss it with anyone. Mother thought that perhaps in her youth grandma had read a romantic novel about a Wanda. The name had never been in the family before, and all her relatives thought it was dreadful. Grandmother was sort of the maverick in her family of seven brothers and sisters.

"Your grandmother," mother used to say affectionately, "was just a bit of a nut."

I didn't think so, but I knew what she meant. Grandma was a very bright progressive type who wrote—and sold—poetry when she was young, and in her later years supported an invalid lawyer husband by working on her small-town newspaper as a social columnist —a job she detested. She lived in Virginia, and every so often we'd visit her. She was a real hug-and-cookies kind of grandmother. She died when I was nine. I never knew my grandfather because he'd died when I was two. But grandma, old and feeble and oh—all that trouble old ladies have—still had the newspaper job when I knew her. She looked as if a puff of wind might blow her away, but she still got on the phone and called all the other old ladies, and some young Junior League ones, and then typed out that column. She thought it was silly, and that attitude, along with her cookies and hugs, was what I found so endearing. I really loved her.

Her name had been plain Elizabeth Smith, which she got out of by marrying my grandfather Drew Westerley. My own private suspicion about mother's name is that grandma used it just because she liked

the sound of Wanda Westerley! I could be wrong, because the name is so awful and grandma's poetry was
so good. Of course, I now realized there was the blue-
bordered card. Maybe they'd been expecting a Walter
or Wendell.

Anyway, she'd made no bones about the next name,
Rowena. Grandma was enamoured of *Ivanhoe*. And
Glad was just a contraction of a favorite sister's name,
Gladys, and because she was "glad" about mother. I
guess being a poetess she couldn't help fooling
around with names.

We stopped at New Dorp, and what with feeling
that little card in my pocket, I couldn't help getting
terribly sentimental about grandmother. How had she
felt at 8:15 P.M. all those years ago? Proud? Happy?
Loving the baby, and with all sorts of plans for it?
She'd been "glad"! What would she think of that little baby now!

What would she think of me and my predicament?
Waves of self-pity flooded me. I pulled out the card,
looked at it, and wished I had a picture of the Taj
Mahal to paste over it. That's the kind of inspiration
that makes you giggle and choke and leaves you miserable afterwards.

We rattled on and the light outside got brighter and
brighter while I got gloomier and gloomier as the last
vestiges of that sick hangover faded away. It had been
better before, throbbing, and letting in dark thoughts.
Now everything was so real it hurt, and by the time
we reached Atlantic, the stop before Tottenville, I
realized what was going on. I was trying to go back to
the same scene. I wanted *yesterday*—rain, storm, and
all! And it wasn't going to *be*!

As we reached Tottenville I knew the other part,
too. Scorpio wasn't going to be there. I could wish all

I liked. I could pray, cross my fingers, turn around three times—but I might just as well turn around and go back. This whole thing was a stupid, emotional, wasted trip.

But there were twenty minutes to wait, so I got off and slowly inched along down the ramp. The raincoat was hot, but I didn't want to take it off because I was wearing my dark red cotton velour "here-I-am-look-at-me!" mini dress underneath. With sneakers! The feel of that dress next to my skin, and my naked feet in the sneakers, was just horrible. Embarrassing. I mean, I embarrassed myself! What had I had in mind, anyway?

I didn't even want to look at the bar again, much less go in. At least it was real. It existed up there, along with the weeds in Tottenville. I stood among them for a while, sniffing pollen, gazing stupidly at some sail boats off the end of the island. Then I felt even stupider! I had forgotten that I could at least leave Wanda's birth date up there for Scorpio. I didn't have any extra paper, though and didn't want to leave the actual card. That would have felt too private and sort of against grandmother, who was very much in my thoughts. I was too tired to walk around looking for a stationery store, and I thought the bartender might have a pad or something. So I made myself walk up the hill, open the door, and go in.

MIRACLE! MIRACLE!

He was there!

It was so totally unexpected that I was disappointed. Do you know how these things go? It's crazy, but I was sorry to find him! It took me a whole long time, listening to the old music—"There'll Be Blue Birds Over the White Cliffs of Dover"—to stir myself and get into a different mood so I could walk over to him.

He was at the same table with his back to me, and he looked, at least from the rear, exactly the same. He even seemed to have collected yesterday's aura of gloom around him. (Which was really dust motes caught by the sun in the window, but I thought he could magically summon his own dark halo!)

Great! I was into it again. I walked over, sat down, and gave him mother's card without saying a word.

"Aha!" he looked at the card and then up at me. "The mysterious Wanda!" He got out his little book and checked, without a word of real greeting to me. "Yep, Capricorn rising! That's some combination with Gemini!"

"She's a filing fiend," I offered. The words came out with remarkable ease, considering all I'd been through that morning. "Does that mean anything?"

"Sure," he fished out a pencil, looked up some more stuff in his book, scribbling on a paper napkin. "Capricorn risings are terribly finicky. File clerks, researchers. Go into her bureau some day and you'll find everything in neat piles. They even file their clothes."

I watched him, hardly able to believe he was really there. I wanted to reach over and touch him, to make sure, but he was so deeply engrossed with mother. It didn't matter. I began to feel a lovely rumble in my middle, just being near him. He was so handsome in a dark, brooding way, that I didn't even mind the sunshine pouring in the window.

"Support your USO! USO! USO!"

I jumped at the bird's loud croak, having forgotten where I was. Nothing was on the juke box now, and there was only one man at the bar.

"Saturn in Scorpio, mid-heaven . . . ah, ha, ha!" he said excitedly. "Jupiter in Capricorn, Moon in Taurus . . ." Suddenly he frowned at me, "Are you sure she didn't *plan* for this trip?"

Plan to be the missing sunshine? My own words came back to me. "No!" I gasped. "That is, I don't know. Maybe she did. No—she couldn't have. No, she just split, I think."

"On American Express, overnight! India, here I come!" He grinned to himself, and kept checking things. "Uranus in Pisces, Neptune in Leo, of course. Ah ha! Mars *and* Venus in Cancer." He paused for quite a time over that. Then he looked up, "They don't get along well, right? That why she split?"

"Who?"

"Wanda and what's-his-name . . . over the hill and dale—"

"Overbrook! He's called Brook."

"Wanda and Brook. Don't make out? Do make out? What?"

He was talking about *my* parents! As if they were kids! I froze, not knowing what to say. "They're . . ." What? A perfect combination? A lousy combination? All my former suspicions about their being in the wrong century and kind of mismatched, came back. Would they have been better together, or worse, in another time, another place? "They're MLU's!" I blurted out.

This went right over Scorpio's head, because he was checking again. "What's he? What's Over—uh, Brook's birthday?"

For some reason I was feeling a little irritation. "May 21," I snapped. "And I don't know the time or year!" This was a bit of misrepresentation, because I could have figured it out. I knew that he was three years older than mother.

"Taurus—Gemini cusp. Oh, well. Trouble no matter how you slice it. The thing I don't get is Wanda.

She's more dutiful, to work and family—sense of law—
Saturn. I don't get this extravagant American Express
bit, unless there're transits. Wish I had my other
book here. Fascinating!"

Why was he so interested in my mother?

Something strange happened just then. I *knew,* with
a sudden loud click, that he didn't think of mother in
middle-aged terms at all! And like a flash, a picture of
the construction guys who whistled at her popped into
my head. Coming right on top of my question to myself, "Are you jealous, Jane?" it was very upsetting.
Then it occurred to me that perhaps for astrologers,
everyone was ageless. He did have the birth card right
in front of him, with that blue satin bow practically
winking up. In fact, the actual baby could have been
gurgling on the table between us! But it didn't make
me feel any better. I wanted him to pay attention to
me! And I still had all these questions. Imagine a
guy who wanted to live in World War Two being so
interested in my mother. Why? And an astrological
nut to boot. Besides being so gorgeous and fascinating that I knew I would go anywhere with him, do
anything, if only he'd ask! Why weren't his questions
about *me?*

By this time I was sick of my mother again. Sick of
thinking about her, questioning her, missing her, sick
of my own emotions. I felt waves of frustration. He
spoke as if she were some contemporary of mine. She
could have been a girl friend—she could have been
Mary!

I whipped off the raincoat to expose *me* in all my
mini-glory, and asked, "How can a *middle-aged* person just drop out like that?" I said it kind of meanly,
just to remind him how old she was.

"Anybody can drop out anytime," he said, not looking at me. "She's not so middle-aged, anyway. Saturn retrograde, then going direct. She's got her best years ahead. Keeps getting younger all the time."

My stomach went into knots. It was true! I remembered the pictures!

"She's attracted to the occult all right, but she's a worker. Works very hard, doesn't she?"

I didn't hear right away, because I was in this mess of conflicting emotions. It's a funny thing, isn't it, the way words can linger, and even though you don't hear them the first time, they can be caught after a minute, just floating there. Some people would say the sound goes, but that isn't true. Some words seem to wait, until you catch up to them.

"Yes, yes," I finally said, "it's true. She does work very hard." Other things were catching up with me, too. Like the fact that everything he'd said so far was true. And what *else* did he know, anyway?

"Why are you so interested in my mother? And how come all this astrology thing?"

He put down his pencil and book and looked at me calmly, "I'm interested in anybody who drops out." He couldn't help the smile then, playing around his mouth, "And particularly a *mother*? To India? And the way she did it. God bless you, Wanda!" He was still grinning as he added, "As to astrology—well it's simple, kid. It works. That's all. It works!"

"Kid!" he'd said. I stared at him, and he was looking at me. Our eyes really held together, and I didn't know what was going on. Scorpios. What had I ever heard about Scorpios? I didn't know much about astrology, but Scorpios . . . They were supposed to be interested in sex, the body. They were sensual or something. Our eyes still held, mine agonized, his remote, calculating. And he didn't even look at the dress.

"Well, *is she ever going to come back?*" Those words came pouring out of me. Believe it or not, but that's what I said.

And it must have sounded awfully breathless and childish, because he was really surprised. His expression changed and he stuffed everything away in his pockets, mumbling, "I'd have to do a lot more figuring. This is surface." He looked at me again and added in a softened way, "Wanda's got Uranus in Pisces. You're Pisces. You've got Gemini rising and she's a Gemini. You've got all the answers to anything you want to know about her already—in yourself."

And immediately he seemed sorry to have said all that. "If you want real answers go to a real astrologer. Or a priest. Find your own guru. I'm just fooling around." Then he stood up.

He wasn't going to leave me, was he? I stood up too, really, I admit it, trying to display myself. If I'd remembered the *sneakers* I would have died! But I didn't. I wasn't even conscious that I had them on. I was all involved with my short dress and the low cut, and the fact that I looked great in it, and why hadn't he noticed? What had I done wrong? What had I said? I thought that he was going to walk off and leave me there. But instead he changed again. He got all tough and abrupt. "Come on, I'm tired of this!"

I followed him out, like a puppy, wondering what he was tired of. Me? But then he wouldn't have said, "Come on." I was really non-compos, I guess, because all I had in mind was staying with him. We stood outside in front of the bar and he asked vaguely, "Want to go somewhere?"

"Sure," I said, hoping it didn't sound too eager. "Where?" I added casually, as if it were just slightly important.

He looked down at me sideways. He was about half a head taller. And he smiled suddenly, a teasing, secretive smile. "India!" It turned into a grin. *"Tibet!"* he proclaimed loudly.

The two young train conductors were just coming up the hill, and looked up in surprise as they heard him. And they looked at me. I quickly remembered to put my raincoat back on. Scorpio grabbed my hand, and we hurried across the street together.

Where was he taking me? From his tone, I gathered it must be a joke, but I couldn't help wondering—and hoping—that maybe he had an American Express card himself. Oh, wouldn't that be lovely—to split like that all of a sudden! In a second I had us out at Kennedy International, then on a plane together, eating fancy dinners and drinking champagne, landing in—No, I didn't want to go to India! We'd go to Switzerland or Tahiti. Or, it didn't even have to be that fancy. We could split by Mohawk to Lake Placid or Saratoga.

I looked at him, hoping to read his plan, but he just pulled me along, humming mysteriously to himself. Across the street and down a half block was a bus stop with an empty bus waiting. Okay, so it was a bus for openers. I didn't care. I'd go anywhere! We waited for the driver to return from wherever he'd gone, and Scorpio didn't say a word. Since he insisted on being so quiet, I tried to just bask in the warm sensation of his young male presence. It was hot, and he was still wearing that plaid wool shirt, so I even got a nice whiff of him from time to time. Like his hands, it was just right. Just male-ish enough and pleasant. I guessed he was going to lure me to some out-of-the-way spot and begin by pointing out the flora and fauna, and maybe tell me allegorical tales of Tibet. But maybe not.

All these background thoughts, plus our conversation, plus being called a kid, plus his not making advances, suddenly led to a terrible question. Could he possibly be one of those guys who preferred older women? Could he possibly be secretly interested in my *mother?* This horrible thought almost ruined everything. He did seem the sort of person who could get interested in somebody from a distance, because of something strange or intriguing about them. It made me feel—peculiar. And sort of dusty, like the weeds here and the plants at home.

But then the driver came, and we boarded the bus along with a group of teen-age boys who were terribly noisy and letting off steam. They threw all their beer bottles into the bushes from the bus windows before we started off. And there was one insurance salesman, I think. I can't imagine what else he might have been.

We sat up front to avoid the teenagers, and that trip was really something. I don't think anybody rides the buses on Staten Island any more than they have to. There was no question of talking because the bus rattled and churned and shook so that it was impossible. The teenagers tried to scream at each other over the rattle-clank-bing-bang, until even they gave up and became gradually subdued. By the time they got off at an orphan home along the way, where I guess they lived, they were as quiet and bowed as old, vagrant monks.

Scorpio kept humming to himself—I could tell by the full look of his throat—as we banged along this strange, bumpy, potholed road. In spite of the sunny day I had the same impression as the first time on the train. Old and new in contrast. Rusted ironworks, discarded boats, a little strip of cemetery only six feet wide squeezed in along the roadside; grand colonial mansions, old houses, modern brick horrors. About a half hour later we came to a quaint old-fashioned village evidently in the middle of reconstruction. The bus stopped and Scorpio took the opportunity to say, "This is Richmondtown. They're recreating the colonial village."

I love old things like that, and I hoped this might be where we were going. I'd loved Williamsburg when we took a trip there. But this wasn't what Scorpio had in mind as "India." When the bus started again I thought we might go on for hours more, but he pulled the bell at the very next stop. We got off at the foot of something called Lighthouse Avenue.

"Where are we going?" I finally dared ask.

"Up the hill," he pointed.

"What's there? Is it another part of the old village?"

"No."

It was a very long hill, getting sharply steeper in the distance. There were some really lovely houses along the way, in a woodsy, suburban setting. Scorpio kept hold of my hand as we trudged up in the hot sun.

"Do you have friends here?"

"Sort of," he seemed amused. "Shut up and walk."

In spite of the fact that I wouldn't have exchanged the touch of his hand for anything, I did get just a little irritated with that mysterious smile. My legs were hurting from the climb, I was out of breath, our hands were sweating, and he kept humming "Song of India" all the way.

Ten

He knew exactly where the bell was, but if I'd been alone it would have taken me some time to find it. This was not an easy place to enter. There were signs outside: NO TRESPASSING. I began to feel peculiar the moment I saw the house, a strange, leaping, many-windowed structure rising above hidden gardens, obscured by foliage and a restraining fence. It did not have the feeling of a casual sightseer's haunt.

Scorpio pulled me along the fence to a gate and pulled an almost invisible string which led down to a bell hung several feet below on a stone stairway. It had the most peculiar, archaic sound—oriental. A resounding tinkle is the best way I can describe it. I looked at the house again and saw that it vaguely reminded me of something. The Potala! That was it, the Dalai Lama's palace. This impression stupified me. A few moments later someone appeared. I was a little dizzy from the long climb in the sun, and not knowing where I was, so I didn't take her in as well as I might have.

She was an older woman dressed in gray or black, who climbed, in a drifting way, up the steps on the other side of the gate. I do remember her smile, and that she greeted Scorpio as if she knew him. They whispered together. I heard "India" and "Mother skipped." I think she said, "Garden first, then come around." She smiled at me, opened the gate, and then vanished down the steps and around a corner.

Scorpio's boots made a loud, cheerful sound as we descended the stairs and turned onto a little cement path.

"Where are we?" I whispered.

"A museum. This is a center of Tibetan art." He wasn't being particularly quiet. We walked past the back of the house to where the gardens started.

A couple of fast questions shot across my mind. "Why did he bring me *here?*" It didn't seem such a joke after all. And, "I wonder if it's really like this in India?" Then just the beginning of another question, "I wonder if mother—"

And then it all stopped. *I* stopped. Something in me crumbled. I could have been a whole statue toppled over suddenly, or a whole lot of fragments just put together. I slipped my hand out of Scorpio's, vaguely aware that it felt damp and warm. I had to be alone right away. I didn't even look to see how he was reacting; I looked at the gardens.

They were really a series of gardens, dropping away from one terrace level to another. Windings and paths everywhere. Blue, scarlet, yellow, pink, orange, and gold flowers. Big statues and little statues tucked away in hidden nooks and crannies. A quiet Buddha sat relaxed under a shady bower of leaves. Small stone cherubs out of childhood dreams waited, peeping and frolicking from behind flowers and plants. They looked up from marble basins or out from friezes set into the walls.

I wandered up and down, from terrace to terrace, around the winding paths, finding more cherubs, Buddhas, angels, elephants, snakes, flowers, at every twist and turn. Seats offered themselves at intervals and occasionally I sat down. I didn't know where Scorpio had gone, and didn't even ask myself. I was just there, walking, looking, sitting, feeling, letting it all move into me. I'd never experienced anything like this before, so it's difficult to describe. But for the first time, maybe, I was in one place and not another. In the present time and not the past or the future. I had no thoughts, no questions, no emotions; I didn't want to *do* anything. I was just there. Now.

I have no idea how long this lasted. It may have been a long time. Eventually Scorpio came to get me, and we left the gardens to go into the museum itself. I felt so quiet inside. I'd never before felt a quiet like that. And I wasn't at all interested in the museum. I don't believe we stayed more than a minute, it seemed so dead after the gardens. There was one huge room stuffed with bronze bowls and statues and dusty hangings, and lots of Buddhas and Tibetan furniture and art. Simple things caught my attention: the white scarfs draped over the hands and in the laps of some of the Buddhas. They looked fresh and living. Later Scorpio told me that they were left by Buddhists who came here.

We left and took a quick glance into the building next door which was the library. Although it had a soft, rather lovely feeling, and seemed to house a remarkable collection of books, I still didn't want to go in. I waited outside the door, looking at the gardens while Scorpio went in and said goodbye to the woman. Then he came out, and we walked back up the steps and out onto Lighthouse Avenue.

I was still in this very quiet, peculiar state, and we didn't talk at all. I felt the walk down the hill in a different way, until we arrived at the bottom where we'd left the bus. There, with the glare of the setting sun striking our faces, and the heat of the dust rising around my ankles, I began to move inside and "come to," old, normal Jane. Although to this day I can't explain the paradox. Why I felt like Jane "coming to" at the foot of the hill, but like someone else *really* "coming to" up in the Tibetan gardens.

Maybe I've skipped over a lot of this, and I'm sorry. But it was such an important experience—it took forever, but it was so fast! And I've run across things like this in books before, and I know it's irritating. But when something like that really happens, it really happens that way. If you're trying to be honest, you just can't describe it. If I went on and on, I know it would be a big lie.

But down there in the sunset everything changed. I was hot, all my memories came rushing back, and I got very tense. Just up the road, within easy walking distance, was Richmondtown. Something I couldn't put my finger on was bothering me. I wanted to get rid of everything suddenly. The memories, even the garden experience.

"Come on!" I squealed to Scorpio. "Let's go to Richmondtown."

He frowned at me almost as if he were disappointed. "You go. I'll see you."

And he started walking off the other way!

"Where are you going?"

There was no response. What could I do? Run after him? His stride was really his! When you watched that walk, there was no question that he knew where he was going.

I toddled after him. "Look—uh—I don't have to see Richmondtown. Uh—what about my mother's chart?"

He stopped at that, and turned to look at me in a

deep way. "Okay, let's talk. But not here."

A bus was coming, he flagged it down, we got on, and believe it or not, went all the way back to Tottenville.

Maybe the obvious thing would have been to ask Scorpio lots of questions. Why had he taken me there? How had he found that place? Who was the woman? Was she a friend?

I already realized that it was a regular museum and guessed it was one of those where people usually made appointments in advance. She probably supervised it, or lived there, or something. But I didn't want to say a word or ask anything about it.

Moreover, I was beginning to move into Scorpio's style of doing things. You didn't have to worry everything to death, asking continual questions, sorting everything out, hashing and rehashing. He seemed to operate on sudden impulses. He had not "lured" me off somewhere. Rather, he had given me something.

He was leaning back in the bus with his legs sticking out and seemed in a cheerful, almost jolly, mood. I had never known anyone whose moods changed so swiftly! As we stopped at Richmondtown to let a passenger off, he asked, "Where were you in 1945?"

"I wasn't here!" I laughed surprised. "What are you talking about, reincarnation?" With him, that wouldn't have surprised me.

"No, I'm talking about stuff—atoms—material. The material that was you. Where was it back then?"

The bus started again. If I'd heard him right, it occurred to me that in addition to everything else, he was *my kind* of whacky person. These were exactly the type of questions that my friends always teased me about. I loved crazy questions like this.

"I don't know where I was," I shouted over the

motor noise. "Maybe I was scattered. Maybe I had to be collected. Where were you?"

Crash! The front wheels dropped into a rut.

"What?" he shouted, grinning.

"Where were you in '45?"

"Here! I'm still here. Hallelujah!" He started to laugh, and then I did, too, because we were the only souls on that bus and the driver must have been breaking all the speed rules. It was impossible to say a word. We gave up and sat, half laughing all the way, until the bus stopped at the top of the hill in Tottenville.

"What do you mean you're still here?" I asked as we got off.

He draped an arm over my shoulder as we crossed the street. "I think all my components were eternally formed in 1945!" He was really expansive about the idea.

"Actually we were both DNA molecules, I guess. But why are you stuck on 1945? I mean, if you've been around *that* long, you could have been here forever." I stopped excitedly at the street corner. "If we've both been DNA molecules or, you know, *memories* in the DNA, or even projections, like a memory of the future—things to come—then we've been here since the beginning of time. If you want to look at it that way, we were here when the world was made!"

He really raised his eyebrows, staring at me. I guess he didn't know what a true nut I am in this direction. It's my very favorite subject, so I kept babbling. "Therefore we have to be eternal, isn't that right?"

We walked on and into the bar. "If we were always here as matter from the beginning of time, or as a memory of the future, then it just follows. We'd have to always be here in the future as matter, or as a memory of the past. Does that mean we're immortal?"

He sort of made me sit down at our table. I repeated my question and then added, "So why do you say you never left 1945? Do you mean you think we're always in all places at the same time? Something like that?"

He gave me a very strange look, "What have you been reading?"

"Everything!" I said excitedly. "I read everything!"

"Obviously!" He smiled, and it made me feel small again.

"Tell me about 1945!" I insisted. "Why that particular year? Is it because of the peace, and the end of the war, or did you die in the Battle of the Bulge?" I was sort of teasing over that, but he looked at me most suspiciously.

"Play 'That Old Black Magic,'" I giggled. I was high as a kite already, just on this kooky, one-sided conversation.

He gave me another suspicious look, went to the juke box, and did *not* put on my request. Instead he played "Lili Marlene" again. He came back with two cognacs, and the bird went off. "Buy war bonds! Buy war bonds!"

And back we were in yesterday. Instant magic!

And guess what! We got potted—*again!* That very night! On cognac!

Eleven

Now here's the thing. I was *determined* to stay with Scorpio all night. So naturally I paid no attention to the small, vague thought of my father that flitted across my mind. When it came, I glanced half-heartedly in the direction of the telephone booth, but after two cognacs it really didn't seem important. I felt smug. And delighted with myself. Which is extraordinary considering that in all the time we'd been back at the bar, I hadn't remembered to take off my raincoat, and I nevertheless thought I was being alluring. And even more extraordinary when you consider that I'd also had that important experience, and although I treasured it, I was also trying to get rid of it!

That's about how it was, except that I didn't get quite as drunk as I had the other night. I was gay, giddy, joyous. And Scorpio was swinging, too, in his own weird way.

"Pisces-Gemini!" he chuckled, chin in his hand, staring at me across the table. "Double fish—double twins. Or is that a redundancy? I'll bet you're redundant! Want to do everything twice, or over? Have a contradictory thought for every thought you have? Want to do two different things at once?"

"Yes, yes," I cried, "you're right!" Of course I was prepared for him to be right about everything, particularly at the end of the evening when he was supposed to suggest that we go somewhere.

"Hah!" he laughed, "I don't envy you. How'd you know about the Battle of the Bulge, anyway?" *That* question sure came from left field, I thought.

"I'm not stupid! I know everything!"

"Everything?" he teased.

"Well, everything you know, I'll bet! Except," I thought this was very clever, "why you are so fascinated with World War Two."

I really thought he was going to hedge, or be mysterious. But he answered promptly and openly, as if it were the most obvious thing in the world.

"Simple! In World War Two everything was crystal clear."

And suddenly, so was I. On a quick intuition, I got it. "You're worrying about the draft, right? And you wish it was World War Two so you wouldn't have any doubts about it!"

He was struck with open admiration. "Pisces!"

"Haven't you been called up yet? Are you 1-A? Think it'll be this year?" Aha! He *had* to be just nineteen, if he was worrying about this. "Why didn't you get a deferment or a 4-F? There are ways to freak those doctors out—or you could even split to Canada."

He said nothing, but his expression told me I'd hit pay dirt. I said, "You see, I am intuitive, am I not?" And took another sip of cognac.

I was learning how to drink! You don't do it all at once, just a little at a time. And then it can go on forever. "So!" I announced, "*if* I'm right about all this, I've guessed your problem. And if I've guessed your problem, we have no more secrets!" I deliberately left Wanda out of this. "Therefore, I do not see why you can't tell me your real name or where you're from, etcetera, etcetera!"

One side of his mouth curled. "Don't push. Let's leave it. We're strangers, Going to remain strangers."

"But that's like a bad movie!" I cried. "We can't be strangers. We already have 'our' song!"

He choked into his cognac. "What's 'our' song?"

I blinked. "Well, 'Lili Marlene'?" And I felt stupid. And *horrible!* Every time I ever heard a World War Two song again—*any* World War Two song—it was going to be "our" song! How ghastly! It was going to kill half the late shows for me.

He was cracking up, over the table, and into his cognac glass. Which was not very romantic of him! And it upset me. "Why do you think everything was so clear back in World War Two?" I asked, to get off the song subject, and with the happy reasonableness of a junior psychiatrist.

"Come off it," he growled, shocking me a little, and getting me back to my true sixteen-year-old self. "Have another drink."

"You're paying for them!" My, I was bold!

He went away and returned with two more to the tune of "Praise the Lord and Pass the Ammunition."

"Okay, let's get it straight, so you'll stop bugging me."

"I'm not bugging you!"

"No, of course not! Only every look—why in hell don't you take off that lousy raincoat?"

I did, smiling deliriously.

"World War Two," he pontificated, "was what someone once called 'a clear and present danger.' That's a nice dress. I like it. Like the color." He took me all in for a minute and then resumed. "Which is why it's a comfortable time to spend one's time in. Whoever had a question about World War Two? Oh, good lord! What am I talking to you about, anyway? Let's go back to materials, components."

"But I already know all about that! We come from the stars. Every atom—even every DNA molecule originally came from the stars. We are really star material. And as far as I'm concerned, we belong up there, not down here. What do you think?"

"Yeah, I agree."

"I just can't figure out your 1945 thing. Why not 1940?"

"It was over in '45," he mumbled, looking down. "And what they'd done they felt good about."

I was smashed. But even so, it was clear to me that he was going through a great big thing about the draft, the war. Maybe it was conscience. He was asking himself what to do. But I'd never heard of *anybody* who went through this in such a big serious way that they'd actually flip back to World War Two to do it!

"I think girls should be drafted, too," I said. "Then I think this whole war thing would be over real fast."

He looked at me.

"But since we aren't and it isn't," I said, "if it really comes down to that, you could skip. Lots of people are skipping. Some of our friends went to Canada, including the parents."

"It isn't that simple," he said quietly, turning the glass round in his hands. "This is a good country." And right away he seemed ashamed to have said such a thing. He shot up to get drinks.

While he was at the bar I desperately tried to think of the magic thing to say. The formula. Anybody who's had a few drinks will know what I mean. You not only want to solve the world's problems, you *can* solve the world's problems. It's just a matter of using the right words.

"Look," I said when he came back. "America is America, but much more important—*you are you!*"

A pained, disgusted look swept over him. "Did it ever occur to you that it's all insane?"

I nodded, "Certainly."

"Did you ever think that we might be living in a madhouse? I mean the whole world? Did you ever consider yourself an *inmate?*"

"Absolutely!" I agreed hazily. But I was still back in my own thoughts, and not really listening. "But what I mean is, you have to do what is right for *you!*"

He looked even more disgusted. "You don't see that your mother's the sane one, do you? You don't dig that."

He was almost hostile, and I didn't want to get into this! Or anything at all about my mother! Suddenly I said—I'm sure it was pretty drunken, "But why are you worrying at all? Don't you already know what you'll do? What does your horoscope say?"

I must have saved my intellectual standing with this, for he smiled. "Aha! Now we approach the question of choice and free will versus fate and determinism! Which answer, I gather you didn't quite see, might just lie up that long hill."

"Right," I interrupted, still not getting his reference to Lighthouse Avenue, "and how about that? How about this astrology bit in connection with free will?"

"Whew!" He ran his hand over his mouth, and I saw I'd spoiled something again. *Why?* What was I doing? He shook his head as if he were infinitely sorry about something, and said numbly, "Want to dance?"

"No! I don't want to dance! I'm not dumb! I'm very, very bright! I'm also extremely well read. I have a bright family who may be a lot brighter than yours! My mother even went to India to solve her problems! And you won't even go to *Canada!*" My voice was rising. "And I can't help it if I'm only si . . . , if I'm not as old as you are. You may be beautiful and know all sorts of weird things, but I don't care how beautiful you are. I'm brilliant!"

"Hello, hello, hello!" Harry the bartender called over to our table. I must have been pretty loud.

Scorpio leaped out of his chair and caught me up and we danced. We danced to "Sentimental Journey" and "Linda" and "Don't Sit Under the Apple Tree with Anyone Else But Me." First we danced wide, then close, while Harry kept telling us that we couldn't dance at all because he didn't have a license, and Scorpio mumbled in my ear, "I know you're brilliant. You're really brilliant!"

And I spouted, "What does it mean that we're all hydrogen atoms in the first place, even before DNA? You know we really are, aren't we?" I mumbled passionately in his ear. Really, he felt marvelous! I began to sing along with the music, like an individual glee club.

Scorpio said, "Let's go!" He left me dangling by the table while he paid for the drinks, then waltzed me out the door, chattering all the way. "Yeah, things were really clear in '45, as your mother could tell you if you'd let her. But you'll never let her, because you're one of the now people. Poor Pisces. Stoned out of her mind and doesn't know anything about the depression."

"I do, too! I do!" I interrupted.

"No you don't. You've got to go through a depression to know it."

"I'm *in* one!" I stated vehemently, hiccoughing. "Nobody's got a depression like mine."

"We're all in one," he said.

"Sure, and I suppose you've been there all the time, like 1945! You're Dorian Grey or the Wandering Jew! You live forever!" I sang out in the moonlight. We were out on the sidewalk, and even the weeds looked drunk, mysterious and romantic. I couldn't have been happier. "You lost all your money in '29 and jumped out a window!"

He steered me across the street, and I forgot all about my intention to spend the night with him, and thought I should protest. "Oh, no, no. I can't go anywhere. I've got that Santa Claus conductor waiting."

You wouldn't dream that he knew who I meant. But he said, "Oh, him? No, he isn't on tonight. We'll wait awhile, and then I'll take you to the train."

Then I remembered. "I don't *want* to go to the train!" I jammed my sneakers on the sidewalk and stood stubbornly. I took the raincoat which he was holding, and flipped it around like a bullfighter's cape. "I'm not going to the train! I'm going to India!"

"Okay, Wanda," Scorpio grabbed my arm and made me march. "We're going to India."

He must have made me walk around for a half hour at least until my head cleared. Honestly, I wasn't too terrible, just very high and giddy and talkative and excited. He wasn't so utterly sober either! Eventually, when I'd calmed down a little, and we were both just pleasantly high, he said, "Okay, let's go."

"Where this time?"

"Didn't you want to see Richmondtown? Let's go to Richmondtown!"

And we did. Back on that very same bus, on that very same road, for the third time that day!

Twelve

While we waited for the bus we sang World War Two songs. We were in a very great mood and it was a long wait. By the time the bus came Scorpio had taught me every verse to "Jolly Sixpence" and I thought it was hilarious. On the bus we started off with the Army Air Corps song, then "Waltzing Matilda," Scorpio's bad German version of "Lili Marlene," and something new to me which I tried to follow, about a town named Oran.

At that time of night—it must have been after midnight—we were the only passengers. The bus driver kept looking back at us with this startled expression. He was a small, pinched, dedicated person, something like—yes, Don Knotts. Finally he timidly began singing, too. We promptly moved up front and sat down right across from him. While the first driver had taken thirty minutes to Richmondtown, and the speed demon on the return trip had cut that to fifteen, this fellow took more than *forty-five* minutes to get there! We didn't pick up one other passenger.

We all sang "Come Back to Sorrento," "Bell Bottom Trousers," "Comin' in On a Wing and a Prayer." Everything. A complete repertoire. The driver never lost that startled expression, but you just knew he was having a tremendous time. Every time we neared a rut or a pot hole, he would slow down and hold up a finger; we would all hold our breaths and go, *"Aaand . . ."*

We had a ball!

Where was daddy all this time in my mind? And mother? Well, Wanda seemed to be riding along with us in some peculiar way, maybe because she was so distant. But Overbrook was right over there in Manhattan, so I thought of him as just absent. Like you raise your hand in school to let the teacher know someone isn't going to be there? He was absent like that, home sick in bed or something. I didn't dare think about him. And poor old Dick, well, he didn't even exist. It was World War Two, the bus driver, Scorpio, Pisces, and the wraith of mommy Wanda.

By this time, my third trip in that bus, I had a directional rattle in my bones to indicate the approach of Richmondtown. I was feeling charitable toward the whole world, even mother. So I suggested we leave World War Two and top all this off, "a la mode," with Wanda's favorite.

We began "Happy Days Are Here Again"—and I thought the driver was going to burst into tears. We sang it with *feeling,* almost as if it were the national anthem. When he stopped the bus he sat there, finishing the song with us, his eyes enormous, and then drove off looking more startled than ever. As if something in his life had changed.

We stood at the bus stop, in the moonlight, watching the bus rattle away, and Scorpio motioned to me, "Shhh."

He was looking, listening. "Are we playing commando?" I giggled.

"Shh, quiet!"

We stood so silently that I could hear every little cricket. Across the street was a lovely old white colonial house with a weeping willow beside it on the lawn. Farther down I could see the water wheel of the old mill and other houses in various stages of reconstruction. Finally he took my hand, and we started walking. I realized that we couldn't go into any of the houses at night; they were closed. But I thought he was going to show me the general scheme of the village. He did point up a hill and whispered that up there was a little print shop, a general store, and the main museum. But we didn't go in that direction. We were heading toward a main highway intersection where I could see a large sign with a map and the story of the restoration.

We had a full moon, and it shone on Scorpio's red shirt and made a white streak along the top of his dark hair. I shivered and he threw the raincoat over my shoulders. We walked on quietly, feeling from their persistent chirping, that the crickets were practically under our feet. I knew the Tibetan museum was in the other direction, so we certainly weren't going there.

When we got to the sign, I stopped to look, and Scorpio pointed out the schoolhouse on the map. "First elementary school in the country," he whispered. "Guess what the sampler quote hanging on the wall says."

"I can't imagine. Learning is wisdom?"

"Nope."

"I give up."

"Coward. You should never give up." His hand, over the back of my shoulders, felt warm and protective.

"I'm a coward and I do give up. How would I know what they put on the walls back then? When was it?"

"Oh, the late 1600's. Make a guess."

"Sit silently and do your work."

"Nope," he smiled.

"Oh come on, I really give up."

"It says, 'TIME HOW SHORT, ETERNITY HOW LONG.' "

And with the rhythm of that echoing, we treaded softly on. Now why had he brought that up, I wondered? It was peculiar for little children, wasn't it? "How old were the children?" I asked.

"Shhh! They were all ages. You know how those first schools were, everyone together in one room."

Imagine seeing that every day of your life! "You mean little bitty children had that staring at them every day?"

"*Shhh!*" He veered off the sidewalk abruptly, we ducked behind some screening bushes, and then out through a thicket of young trees to the back of a house. The area was well shaded, but he still acted as if he expected someone might shine a flashlight on us at any minute. We crept across the grass like a couple of cats and stopped in front of a low, many-paned window. The bottom panes were almost at my feet. Scorpio bent down, easily drew up the window, and dropped down inside. Then his head reappeared, and his hand, as he reached up to help me down.

I sat on the sill, and he caught me by the waist as I dropped down into what seemed to be the basement of the old house. Quickly Scorpio set me aside, closed the window, and with swift, sure movements, taped some dark material over that window and another beside it. It was pitch black now, but there was a sudden flare as he struck a match, and then we had light. First a candle which he held while lighting the wick of an old oil lamp. He turned down the flickering flame, put the candle down on a box, and set the fluted glass top over the oil lamp.

I looked around while he stood, ear cocked, at the window. A gray, plaster-encrusted workman's canvas had been thrown half back on the floor, disclosing a pile of stuff underneath. Blankets, cans of food, a small airline bag, a pile of clothes. "Do you *live* here?" I asked, astonished.

He put his finger to his lips, still listening, and didn't answer. The room was a colonial kitchen, almost completed. The walls were whitewashed, the ceiling beams had been rubbed with dark oil, there was a beautiful old table in the center of the wideboarded floor, and a sideboard against one wall with antique utensils hanging over it. But the floor wasn't finished, and one end of the room was piled with unfinished furniture, workmen's tools, cans of paint, newspapers, brushes.

"I move around," he said, coming back from the window. He dug under the canvas, withdrew a bottle of blackberry brandy, a tin cup, and a tiny transistor radio. "Hungry?" he asked, also producing a can of beans and an opener.

I was, so he got out a fork and spoon—I guess he only had one of each—and opened the can on the table. Then he dug into his "pile" again and pulled out a tight roll of dark material. He pulled the string with his teeth and a sleeping bag unfurled which he tossed casually on the floor. "Sit," he offered.

Now that he was "home" he acted entirely different again—loose, modern. Needless to say I was fascinated. So fascinated that I didn't even have enough sense to ask myself why I was here or what happened next. I just sat down on the bag while he brought everything over. He gave me the fork, took the spoon, and we sat there, passing the can back and forth, sharing the beans together. Then I sat some more and watched him clean off the utensils with newspaper, and put the empty can back, carefully, somewhere under the canvas.

"Got to be careful," he smiled, "can't leave litter." He started to sit down again, then jumped up to put the radio on very low, and brought over the blackberry brandy and the tin cup.

Well, as must be obvious, I was totally, madly in love with him, but now that the moment of testing was at hand, I got nervous. So much for all my romantic and noble resolutions. The moment he was down beside me I started chattering. "Do you really live here?"

"Mm, sometimes," he poured out some brandy in the cup.

"But suppose they found you? Don't they have guards looking in or anything?" I gulped some brandy because I was nervous.

He shrugged. "I like old things." Then he looked around, smiling softly. "Beautiful, isn't it? You should see it upstairs. If I had a way of getting us up there . . . There's a four poster with a real trundle bed underneath. Dormer windows. Feeling of this place seeps into you."

He suddenly took the cup out of my hand, looked at me, put the cup on the floor, took my face in both hands and kissed me. Everything spun around. I thought he was going to go right on. However, it seemed there were certain preliminaries.

Never having been in this situation before I knew nothing about preliminaries, so every single thing he did took me by surprise. I thought he was doing everything just for the sake of doing it, and had no idea this was all just the preliminaries!

I'm really dumb in some areas, as I've indicated before.

First there was the blackberry brandy. Then he fiddled around on the radio trying to get old music, but there wasn't any, so he settled for rock and wanted to *jitterbug*. Someday try jitterbugging to rock—it's impossible! I thought we'd damage or shake those old floorboards, and besides I didn't know how to dance like that, but he tried to teach me, and he was pretty light-footed about it.

I stumbled over the edge of the canvas, and he caught me, and in a gorgeous execution of slow-motion, to this wild rock number, we "melted" all the way back onto the sleeping bag. Together. And he kissed me again, and again. And it was just heavenly—except that I was scared. I thought this was probably the real moment to ask him his name and where he was from, but I couldn't, because he was kissing me. And then I got much less scared, and really didn't care any more, and yet somebody in me kept mumbling "Hm, mm, no, no . . ."

He whispered, "Really no? You sure? Yes or no?"

I was sure it wouldn't make any difference what I said, and the proper thing seemed to be a protest, so I kept saying, "No," in spite of feeling "Yes." And you know what he did?

He said, "Okay," and he didn't leap up or get angry or anything. He kissed me again and then got up. *Then* got up! I think that's incredible!

And of course I was absolutely crushed! I hadn't intended for this to happen at all. I looked at him and felt like saying so—he looked so super-terrific standing by the window in the soft light of the oil lamp, but something stopped me. I don't know what, just some ancient subconscious habit, I guess. And after this moment of horrible indecision, I blurted out, "Well, can't we at least cuddle?"

I can't describe the look he gave me. But after going through some apparently strained moments of his own, he sort of barked, "Not now!"

Did he mean never, or in a minute, or what? I didn't ask. Maybe all females have an intuition about moments when it's necessary to keep quiet. This was one of them. I sat like a sphinx, saying nothing, just thinking how horrible this reversal was. How was I supposed to know things were different with him? Or was it him? Was it this way with everybody today? Did you have to say yes to mean yes, when since the beginning of time, I thought, the word for yes was no?

He bustled around, not looking at me, replacing the radio, bottle, cup, threw down two blankets and got a long skinny board from the corner which he dragged over to the sleeping bag. By that time he was smiling again, and I knew he was going to surprise me with something. He sure did! He put that board down the length of the sleeping bag, and sat down on the other side of it.

I thought there was something mischievous, verging on anger about this. He grinned at me, not such a particularly lovely grin, either. "We now have an appropriate colonial bundling board. You can pretend I'm a Revolutionary soldier, you're a Colonial lass, your patriot parents are sleeping in the next room, and they've kindly given me shelter for the night. This is the way it was done. Sorry I can't offer you a feather bed."

His tone was condescending and it irritated me. "I know all about bundling boards," I interrupted. "And they were higher than this. And besides, I might have been a Tory during the war."

"Good night," he leaned over, patted me on top of

the head as if I were a puppy, and rolled over on his side.

A minute later I whispered, "I—I didn't really mean to say no."

"Yes you did," he mumbled, drawing up his blanket over his head. "Drop it, will you?" He disappeared, a mound under the blanket.

Oh, I was so disappointed! I'd ruined everything! But as I lay there wide awake for a while, a sensation of peace began to steal over me. Even if nothing had happened—and maybe that was best. Maybe Scorpio knew more than I did. Still, I was where I shouldn't be, and that was delicious. I was in a pre-Revolutionary colonial home, on a skinny bit of sleeping bag. Next to my hand I could feel the silky old wide floorboards. It was almost pitch black, but I could sense the shape of the furniture, the rest of the house upstairs.

I might even have "pretended" as Scorpio had suggested. But the warmth of the blackberry brandy, and the blanket, and the lovely old house, and Scorpio's presence on the other side of the board stole over me, and I didn't even know when I fell asleep.

Thirteen

Sometime in the middle of the night I woke up. It might have been closer to dawn because there was a faint light around the table. The moment I opened my eyes I was filled with the most extraordinary elation! I lay there with my heart beating fast, stuffed with a montage of emotions. Why do these incredible understandings come in the middle of the night? And from where? I was in the center of it, and lay there panting euphorically.

I'd done it! I'd run away! And if it had happened inadvertently, so what? I was here! That sampler in the schoolroom could have been on this very wall, in this kitchen. TIME HOW SHORT. ETERNITY HOW LONG. That message—think of it! Practically next door to "Tibet." And Tibet—think of it! Just next door, up the hill. I didn't have to be jealous of mother any more. Or anyone. I had my own private India! And Scorpio—my own private guru! Better than guru! And my own private old house. Best of all, I was just like the rest of my family now. I'd run away! I was free! I'd stay here forever with Scorpio. We'd get married. Girls younger than me got married all the time—in the Ozarks—in colonial times. Oh, heaven! And if he was due to be drafted I'd make him skip to Canada, with me! We'd find another restored village and move into an old house. Oh, it was so completely, totally beautiful! It was like science fiction. We'd live in the past in the present. Maybe we could really step back, find the secret of time travel, study things like Time How Short. . . . I was so excited I didn't think I could go back to sleep. I closed my eyes, battered by the beauty of everything.

Then at dawn, the real dawn, Scorpio woke me up again. "Come on, and be very quiet." His hair was mussed and his eyes sleepy as he jiggled my shoulder.

I struggled up under the blanket, a little stiff and cold on one side where the sleeping bag had ended, and I'd been on the floor. I smiled at him. "Do we have to get out for the day?" He nodded.

"Do you have anything else I could wear?" I was thinking of an old pair of pants and maybe one of his shirts, to go with my sneakers. I had a vision of us slinking through the weeds all day until it was time to come back for the night.

He frowned impatiently. "Just put on your coat." He helped me up, and I watched while he rolled up the mattress and blankets. Then he removed all his possessions from under the canvas, stuffing them into the little airlines bag. Candles, can opener, shirts, a pair of shoes.

"Can't we come back here tonight?" I gasped.

"We!" He looked at me.

"Yes. I didn't think you had to move this stuff all the time. How come it was all here last night?"

"They'll be working here today," he said. "Anyway, you have to go home."

Home! This was home! "I want to stay with you! I don't want to go back!"

"Come on, it's too early in the morning!" He lifted the sleeping bag, blanket roll up to his back. "Here, hold this for me, will you?"

I held it in position while he fastened it with

straps around his shoulders. "I'm definitely staying with you," I stated.

"You can't. I move around. And you're a minor."

"I'm *not!*" I protested.

"You're a minor and a virgin, and you're not going to get into trouble. Or get me into trouble."

"But what about last night? If you knew I was a minor, how come it didn't matter last night?"

"Shhh!"

"Besides, things will be different from last night!"

"Oh no they won't. Duck down, will you?" He was taking the dark material off the windows. It really was just dawn, with only a few pale streaks outside. He folded one piece, then the other. It was amazing how small he managed to make them. Then he put them in last on the top of the bag, and zipped it shut.

"You don't have to worry about not being strangers," I insisted. "We can be strangers forever. I agree with you. Maybe I didn't say so before—"

"Shut up and keep out of sight. I have to open the window."

"If you don't let me stay with you, I'll tell you my name!" I threatened.

He looked at me.

"I'm sorry." But it was still right on my tongue. He was angry though, and looked hard, so the impulse subsided.

He pushed up the window, climbed out, and then bent down to help me up. I put my foot on the wainscoting for a toe hold while he lifted, and bumped my head on the sash getting out. It really hurt, but he didn't seem to notice. He closed the window and then we crept away, the way we had come last night. Even after getting out on the highway he still seemed cautious. We started to walk in one direction and then another, when he suddenly stopped. "No, it's too long a walk. Look, you'd better go back to the bus stop. I don't want to be seen around here so early in the morning."

"What's too long a walk?" I asked quickly. He was practically pushing me off.

"To the next stop. I was thinking we could pick up the bus there and you could take the train back from Tottenville. But it's too far."

"No it isn't. Let's go!" I wanted to stay with him as long as I could because I had a horrible feeling that I might have ruined all my chances, and wanted an opportunity to make it up.

"Come on then," he said, and we really loped along that highway, as fast as we could go, away from Richmondtown. "Put your coat back on." He frowned when he noticed I was taking it off. "And why don't you put on the scarf, too, and the glasses?"

"You don't have to worry! Nobody knows where I am, I don't need a disguise." Besides, I didn't want to look so lousy near him. I wanted to be pretty.

"Put it on!"

He was really uptight. We marched along in silence, and I wondered if he was the type who needed coffee in the morning. "Is there a coffee shop around here?"

"No."

"Maybe we could find one?"

Silence.

"Maybe if we went back to that Tibetan place the woman could give us breakfast? I'd like to go back there. Couldn't we talk to her? Maybe look in the library?" I was pulling out everything I could think of to delay us. We reached the next stop and waited. He said nothing.

The bus finally came and I followed him on. "I have a wonderful idea! Maybe you could come to the city with me today, and we could see a flick."

Nothing, all the way to Tottenville. I thought, "I don't have to go home. Why should I go home? He can't tell me what to do." I could follow him around, stick to him like a leech, but I was afraid of losing him. Maybe I should be light about it, treat everything like a joke. But I *had* to know if I'd ever see him again.

When we got off the bus he adjusted his blanket roll, looked around for a moment, and then smiled at me. It was a sudden, very nice, sweet smile. Open, friendly, and warm. "Okay, Pisces. We're home safe."

My heart leaped. "Then I can stay with you? Are we going to stay in Tottenville?"

"I don't know where I'll stay, but you're going home."

"Why don't we go to the bar?"

"It isn't open yet. Go on. Go down to the train. They run fairly often in the morning. You won't have long to wait."

I must have looked just awful, because he said, "What on earth is the matter?"

"What about you? Where will you be? Will I ever see you again?" There, it was out, in spite of me.

"Of course!"

"*Where?*"

"Right there," he seemed astonished, pointing across the street.

"Really? You'll be there?"

"Sure, off and on." He studied me curiously. "Look, Pisces, I'm not saying good-bye forever."

"Honestly?"

He laughed. "You think I want to get rid of you? I do! I do! Go *home!*" But he took my hand, only to drop it because a lot of business commuting types were suddenly appearing around us on their way to the train. "Hey, come on, I'll see you again. I'm not drafted, or dropping out. At least, yet. Pisces! I *do* have a sister!"

It was the very first personal thing he'd told me and it couldn't have been worse! "I'm not your sister!" I panted.

"I know that."

"I'm nothing like a sister, nothing, *nothing!*"

"Cool it!" he informed me in no uncertain terms. When I subsided he said, "I'm perfectly aware that you're not my sister. That's not what I meant." He looked around, and then bent down and kissed me. Not a sisterly kiss!

"See ya," he straightened up, walked away.

Somebody whistled. I whirled around. It was a young man with a tin lunch box on his way down the hill. He was grinning. And Scorpio was drifting off into the middle-class woodlands of Tottenville, and I had nowhere to go except down the hill to the train.

Fourteen

The train was busier, but it was still too early for it to be really full. Right after we passed Atlantic, guess who came into the rear car and looked as if he'd found a missing treasure.

"Ah ha! And what are we doing coming back from Tottenville so early in the morning!" His cherubic face dropped into sudden long lines. He plopped down on the seat beside me. "Miss Jane Elizabeth Andrews! I do hope you haven't been up to anything you shouldn't have been up to?"

Can you imagine how that sounded to me? The last I knew of this man was being stone drunk under an umbrella with him, and talking about a garden, and now he was calling me by *name?*

His Santa Claus face was roundly disturbed. "Jane —are you all right?"

Saucer-eyed and small-mouthed, I stared at him, "Naturally."

His blue eyes peered at me under a tangle of worried gray eyebrows. "Really? Nothing untoward has happened?"

"Nothing—untoward—at all!" I gasped, glad that I read a lot.

He smiled, so anxiously and sweetly, that I suddenly felt like the princess in *Curdie.* "I'm all right!" I squeaked at him.

"I'm so very glad, my dear!" he patted my hand.

He had reminded me of—oh, *everything*—so suddenly, that I almost burst into tears. He kept patting my hand. "You know, I once had an aunt with these peculiar faculties. She knew things before they happened, and it was terrible. She would call us up in advance . . ." He stopped to open the doors at the next station and then sat down again. "My mother was terrified of her and of the phone ringing. Eventually she didn't answer it at all. It created many family problems. I've been thinking it's a good thing that your mother and my aunt didn't live in Puritan New England. They might have burned as witches at the stake. We have a lot to be thankful for. Oh, hello Mr. Ball! All over your flu?" He jumped up to speak to someone sitting down the aisle.

I was frozen. "Burned at the stake?" *What had I told him? What had I said?* I had been drunk. Witches, Wanda, oh, lord!

He came back. "Hi," I smiled weakly.

"Look, Jane, I wouldn't worry about mother if I were you. She will probably come through this A-okay, as they say. I should definitely pay attention to myself."

"I am."

"And not go on these midnight prowls, my dear. That is if you are going on midnight prowls, or whatever you're doing. I do hope you have good friends in Tottenville. The world is not a safe place, sad to say. You don't know what might be lurking around the corner. Oh, tickets! Blast! Nuisance!"

He had to get up to collect them and left me sitting alone. I had the impression that he really resented the whole economic aspect of the train. Tickets, money. He had a word for everyone, and left them all smiling and lots more cheerful. What was he, anyway? The soul doctor of the Tottenville railroad? He seemed to think I was in special need of his services this morning.

"You see this wire on the windows, Jane?" He was back again. "Now I remember when it wasn't needed. In those days it was a rare boy who ever threw rocks at a train window. That's what I mean about the world not being as safe. Look! Look down the street. That's where I lived as a boy for many years before the depression. Before we moved to Brooklyn. Your mother must have been a little girl then. It was a hard time. I hope your family didn't suffer too much?"

"Uh, they lost a lot," I mumbled.

"Did they live in New York?"

"No, my mother grew up in Virginia."

"Lovely place! Is she old enough to remember the war well?"

"Sure. Were you in it?" I asked him.

He chuckled, "I was too old. I'm much older than your mother. My, that was a different era! I suppose your father served?"

"He was in Special Service."

"Oh, yes. Whoops! Excuse me!" He jumped up for Dongan Hills, having nearly forgotten it.

He'd gone into that family discussion so slickly that I suddenly realized he could have fished my father's name from me. Having a minute to think, I saw that I'd have to be careful. He seemed so concerned about me that I just knew it wasn't beyond the bounds of probability for him actually to call my father. Or, did he already know his name? He knew mine! And I didn't remember what I'd told him. Maybe he even knew about Scorpio!

I was quite nervous when he returned, and something else. I wondered where I was going. I didn't mean or want to go home at all!

But he didn't fish for more information, he just chatted cheerfully. "Well, we have another lovely day! Not too warm for comfort. What do you plan to do today when you get home? You do seem a little tired. I meant to tell you something before—now when was that? Day before yesterday, I believe."

I was shocked. It had been only two days! And it seemed like a million years. He watched me, smiling in a comforting, cozy way. He sat in that old-fashioned manner, each hand resting on a plump, blue-uniformed knee.

"When one has imbibed too much, my dear, there's a little remedy that helps, and that's aspirin. It's so much better not to imbibe at all, but of course I know the world isn't simple. You young people today have a difficult time, and it's quite understandable. What I wanted to suggest was not only a little aspirin, but a nice soothing bath when you get home, and a little sleep. A little sleep does a world of good. And you mustn't worry about your mother. I know everything is going to be all right, and you're going to be just fine."

". . . lovely, wonderful, fine . . ." He went on like that all the way to St. George, and by the time I got off the train there was no question where I was going. *Home!* I felt so soothed and comforted, he could have been rocking me in a cradle. And I also felt so old-fashioned and lovely. Like a nineteenth-century heroine who was just caught up in a lot of strange experiences not of her own doing at all. He was like balm; the wise Santa Claus who watched over me from the secret room in the attic upstairs. My fairy godfather!

So imagine my surprise after I'd gone all the way up to our neighborhood, sustained by this lovely warm feeling inside, and was walking calmly down our side street, to notice that there seemed to be a police car following! I looked over my shoulder—and looked again—but it didn't go away. What's more, the two cops in the front seat were taking me in from head to foot. Now cops do *not* stare at you like that! And I had on my complete disguise outfit anyway, and was nothing to stare at. I was my invisible self, I thought. Something about this sort of scared me, so I hurried on, and the car hurried, too, matching speed but staying a little behind. From between Lex and Third to Second, to First, to York, and right along to our house near East End. They had to be going to the mayor's mansion, I told myself.

But when I walked up our steps, the car pulled to the curb and stopped. They were still watching me. I dashed inside, and unlocked our door. My father was on the phone in the living room, and when I walked in he gave me a look I don't like to remember.

The door slammed shut behind me. "Never mind," he said. "She just walked in." He listened to something and said, "Yes, thank you very much. I certainly will. Sorry to trouble you. Right, and thanks again."

I was suddenly so frightened I started to shake. Out the corner of my eye I noticed a letter on the table, and picked it up. But my hands were shaking so hard I couldn't open it, or even see it.

There was a loud, authoritative knock on the door. My father hung up and I shrank back as he passed me to open it. He didn't bother to look through the peephole, he flung it wide to let in the two cops. They were young and good-looking and looked as if they ought to be smiling, but their faces were stiff as masks. They took everything in. Me, my father, the apartment, everything. Just as if looking answered questions. They really scared me. Then one of them said, "Mr. Andrews?"

"Yes, come in."

"This your daughter, Mr. Andrews?"

"Yes, this is Jane. I've just spoken with your precinct captain and canceled the call. Where did you pick her up?"

"We didn't, Mr. Andrews. She seemed to be on her way home, and we followed to make sure she'd get here."

"Where was she coming from?"

"We spotted her between Lex and Third."

"She might have been coming from the subway," the other cop said. "That right, miss?"

"Yes," I whispered, wondering how they'd recognized me in all my junk.

"You don't know whether she was coming from uptown or downtown?" my father asked.

"No, sir, we couldn't tell you that. She was walking down your street, and we spotted her from your description of the raincoat, scarf, and glasses. She seemed to be coming home."

There was a silence while both the cops and my father stared at me. I couldn't stop trembling. I hadn't known my father even knew I wore this stuff. And they looked so serious. One of the cops noticed the ring on my finger. "Has your daughter worn a wedding band before?"

Daddy said, "Put out your hand, Jane!"

I thrust it behind my back. "This doesn't mean anything! I wear it so people won't bother me. I've always worn it. You've seen me wear it before. It's from the dime store."

"That true, Mr. Andrews?"

Why didn't he ask *me?* I was there! I couldn't stand

the way they talked about me in the third person, as if I didn't exist. They even looked at me like that, like I was a statistic!

"I believe I have seen it before," said my father.

Another silence while they looked between us to see if *he* was telling the truth. Then my father tried to smile. "Well, thank you very much. You're certainly alert. I appreciate the way you handled this."

"That's it, then? Nothing more you want us to do?"

"I think not. She was evidently coming home."

"If you want to put her under court jurisdiction, you'll have to go down and get a PINS: Person in Need of Supervision. You know about that?"

"Yes, that's all been explained."

I froze, absolutely horrified.

"All right, then, Mr. Andrews. If you have any more problems, you can always call." They turned to go and my father went to open the door. I was so petrified that I was only dimly aware I had one thing to be grateful for: he hadn't asked me where I'd been *in front of them!*

He had his hand on the knob, when we all saw it turn with an outside click from the latch, and in walked—*Dick!*

He stopped short seeing our father, the two policemen, and me.

He looked *awful!* He had a sallow tan that had peeled in spots a long time ago, leaving pink areas and large splotchy freckles on either side of his nose. The blue circles under his eyes which he'd inherited from mother were worse than ever because the area around his eyes was stark white where he'd worn sunglasses. He needed a shave and his yellow beard was prickling through the sallow tan on his cheeks and coming out below his nose. His hair was bleached from the sun and looked like sand. Maybe it was matted with sand, because it was plastered down horribly on top of his head, but stuck out down and under his ears, and around his collar. He was wearing a tan suede shirt that laced up the front and was stiff and spotted all over where he'd sweated in it. He looked as if he hadn't been near a shower in weeks. His black cotton pants were also spotted all over and the pockets were torn. And no socks or shoes. He was wearing leather sandals with his dirty bare toes sticking out. And he didn't have a suitcase or even an airlines bag. He was carrying a ragged, pink-striped paper *shopping bag!*

The policemen really looked at him. And looked at him. And seemed to be trying to decide something. They looked at my father, who was very neat in his Brooks Brothers suit, and who was gazing at Dick just as hard as they were. Anybody could see the wheels turning. Were they or were they not going to search him for grass? But they remained absolutely deadpan serious. One said, "Is this another member of the family, Mr. Andrews?"

Very reluctantly my father admitted, "My son, Richard."

"Okay, Dick," one cop said very slowly. Dick's hand was on the knob. "Okay, fella, you can come in. Everything all right?"

All the color on Dick's face, the spots, the blue circles, had taken on an ashen hue. Very gingerly he stepped in and let the door close behind him. "Sure . . . everything's . . . just . . . fine . . ."

"Has he been giving you any trouble, Mr. Andrews?" asked one cop very politely.

My father looked at the ceiling. "No," he said slowly, "Dick has been away."

The cop turned to my brother. "Just getting home, fella?"

Dick nodded very slowly. I was going crazy! Everything was in slow, slow motion!

"Have a nice trip, kid?"

Dick stared and the cop smiled—*first smile!* "Where've you been, Richard?"

Oh, lord, it was threatening! Now I was terrified for my brother!

"California," Dick said hoarsely. He carefully lowered the shopping bag to the floor.

The cop eyed it and smiled again, "Bring back any sea shells?"

Dick still had his hand on the handle. I was afraid he might clutch it up again, because of what might be in it. But he let it go and straightened up, smiling weakly. "No, just clothes. Uh, you can look if you want."

"That's okay, kid," said the cop.

They looked around the apartment again and then nodded at each other. "Well, everybody seems to be home in one piece. Nobody else missing, is there, Mr. Andrews?"

I closed my eyes. He wasn't going to say it, was he? He *couldn't.*

"No!" said my father, "And thanks a lot. Thank you very much!"

Just before they went out, the cops got human and smiled back at us. "Don't give your parents any trouble, you two. Okay? Take it easy."

And daddy shut the door and turned to look at us.

Fifteen

I'm not sure that I want to go too thoroughly into the scene that followed. It was new for us, and new for my father, too. But I didn't know that. I felt so crushed and threatened by the police, and by my father, knowing he had called them, that I didn't realize it was horrible and disgusting and strange for him, too.

And then there was Richard. Although he had gone through his share of adolescent stages, the worst of them was never like this! I was so shocked at his appearance myself I never thought what my father might be feeling. It was all terrible. The police, Dick, me: it made the apartment look different. Made us all act differently.

My father was hopping mad. And I don't say that to be funny or to lighten the situation. He actually did hop, and it was the worst thing I'd ever seen. It was particularly horrible coming right after the cool way he had thanked the policemen. He was stiff and tight and jerked up and down on his heels and shouted. I shriveled up inside, thinking the neighbors were going to come. He'd never lost control like this before. In fact, it wasn't my father.

He wanted to know where I'd been, and I was so scared I couldn't answer. Finally I got out something about walking around all night, and he didn't believe me, and I couldn't think of anything else, so I stuck to that like a broken record. "I don't know where. I was walking all over the city. I don't know! The Bronx, I think. All around. I just walked. I don't know, I *walked!*"

Then, shaking with rage because he couldn't dig anything else out of me, he turned on Dick and wanted to know how he had gotten home.

Well, this was really bad. It couldn't have been worse. Dick was still in the dark, you see. He hadn't lived through all the, oh, peculiar moods and qualities of the time since mother had skipped. I don't know what he'd expected to find when he walked in, but it certainly wasn't me in my disguise cowering from two cops, or my father—this stranger, he must have felt—in an almost hysterical rage.

Dick innocently gasped out that he had borrowed the money to fly home from Los Angeles, and my father, shouting, asked how, who from and how was Dick going to *pay it back?*

That did it. It was the expression on Dick's face. Like me, he was so stunned that he couldn't think of anything, either. His face sort of hung there staring at my father with the answer right in it. *Father* was supposed to pay it back, of course.

I was petrified. Dick was, too. He had to back up because father was advancing. I won't mention the language he used. I didn't know he knew such language. Maybe it came back from his old Army service in time of need, I don't know. After he finished swearing at Dick, he shot these horrible questions at us. Who or what did we think he was, anyway? Mr. Rockefeller? This was not the United States Mint! What did we expect? Was he some poor sap lying down on a doormat for his family to walk all over?

Then he shouted that he was *not* Mr. Moneybags, this was *not* Fort Knox, and as far as he was concerned Dick could get out of his house for good—and so could I, for that matter.

I was trembling, Dick was breathing heavily in jerks and starts; my father got right up close, staring Dick in the face, so tight he was like a ramrod. Then he suddenly whirled around, marched to the door, and yelled at us that we could take care of our own lives! He was finished! He slammed the door so hard a print fell off the wall. We heard the outside door slam, shaking the floors, and then his steps, rapid, hard, going away.

I think it was everything coming at once. I think that if it had been just me, even after having been out all night, he wouldn't have been like this. Angry, yes, but not this. I think it was Dick coming in at just that time. And the way the cops had looked and acted with him. I think in a funny way that my father's whole life fell apart just then. But at the time neither of us thought of this. We only knew that our MLU had turned into a monster and walked out on us.

I picked up the print and hung it up again. The glass hadn't broken. Then I looked at Dick. We didn't know what to say to each other. He was still shaking, and he slowly let himself down on the couch, and looked around his "home." He got up, looked out the window, and then sat down again, staring at his filthy toes.

I was suddenly drained. I'd never been so tired in my life. I wished with all my heart that I'd never come home, that I'd stayed, even just drifting, around Tottenville . . . that I was with Scorpio right this minute.

I didn't want to start talking to Dick right away, and I think maybe he felt the same way. That letter was lying on the floor next to the end table where I must have dropped it. I picked it up, and when I saw who it was from, I sat down next to my brother and we read it silently together.

Dear Brook, Jane, and Dick, (hopefully)

It is quite hot here, but there are large shade trees outside my window, and our spacious central room catches the cross breezes and is very pleasant. Dick—if you're there—I thought of you today when I saw my first elephant! (Remember your nine-year-old interest in them?) He was being ridden along the road in back of our bungalows, and I don't know where he was going. Maybe to clear trees. Miss Nyam says they seldom come near the grounds of the property here, so it was rather unusual—and he was beautiful.

Jane—I've learned to make several interesting Indian dishes, having volunteered for kitchen work. The preparation takes ages, but maybe that's the best part. We're up very early in the morning, and it's a long day with many demands throughout, which is why I haven't been able to write more frequently. I'm sorry, dear.

Brook, you could do something for me if you would, please. Let Miss Hanley at the office know that the Webster file is in *Mr. Kramer's* office. I forgot to tell her when I left, and don't want her wondering too long, in case she hasn't yet found it.

I must leave this now. I do hope everything is working out well, and untangling itself at home. There's very little time left in this sequence, so I probably shan't write again. Don't be concerned about time; I'll be there. My love to you all.

                                                    Mother

I guess it was because I was so tired. I don't know, but as I sat there beside Dick, the tears just started rolling out. He roughly patted my head, and I cried harder, and at the same time I couldn't help noticing that he actually smelled, and that made it worse.

He finally pulled himself up, leaving the letter in my lap, and said his first words to me. "I'd better take a shower."

At any other time it might have been funny. I nodded, and sat there staring at the sheet of paper all the time he was showering and shampooing and shaving and finding other things to wear. I could hear him moving around, and that was a whole lot better than yesterday when I'd been alone! It gave me courage to read the letter again. In fact I read it over and over. By the time he came back, cleaner, and looking *much* better, I'd worked myself up into another terror.

"Why don't you go clean up, Jane?" he frowned. I was still sitting there in my raincoat.

"No, look, look!" I waved the letter at him.

"I read it."

"No you didn't! Neither one of us did. You don't know what it *says!*"

"I read it! I know what it says."

"Look at the end of it again."

Just to humor me, I guess, he snatched up the letter and looked. "So?" he asked impatiently.

"So, what does it say?"

"It says what it says. What's your problem, anyway?"

"That's it! It doesn't say what it says. It says something else." I grabbed it back from him and quoted, " 'No time left in this sequence.' What sequence? What's she talking about? This particular life? The end of this life sequence?"

"Oh, for God's sake, Jane!"

"No! They do talk like that. Don't humor me! You don't know. They believe in reincarnation and all that."

"Who believes?"

"Hindus! It's part of their religion."

"Well, but we don't know what mother believes. She's always said nobody knows about that really. It's the other things that interest her."

"How do you know what she believes *now?*" I cried. "And maybe it isn't just believing—maybe she *knows* something. And look," I read again, " 'Don't be concerned about time—I'll be there.' What kind of time is she talking about? Universal time? Eternity? And she'll be here, even after the *end of the sequence?* If not in the flesh, in the spirit? That's what I mean."

He stared at me and grabbed back the letter. I was praying that he'd tell me I was crazy, nuts. But he didn't. He frowned, read it again, and looked puzzled himself. I started to reach for it again, but he whipped it away and folded it up neatly, making exact creases.

He thoughtfully laid it back on the table. "I don't think so, Jane. Let's not worry about it, anyway." Looking at me, he seemed to have a second thought, and put the letter in his pocket. Probably so I wouldn't read it again.

His circles were still awful, but otherwise he was a different person! He'd put on a clean blue shirt and tan pants, and shoes. It made me remember that my mini dress was under the coat, and I didn't want him to see me in it.

"What if she doesn't come back?" I whispered, drawing the raincoat around me.

"Oh, she'll come back, eventually."

"What if *he* doesn't come back?"

This was probably a lousy thing to do, to present Dick with so many problems so fast when he was so tired and had just found *himself* owing all the money instead of my father. But I was so worried myself. "Who did you borrow the money from?"

He tightened up, "I called Mark Landauer."

Oh, dear! Mark was a very slick kid who always had lots of money, and Dick had often borrowed from him, but always paid back—or at least father did. We both knew that if Mark didn't do anything about it, Mark's father sure would. This was distressing.

"How are you going to pay it back if Daddy doesn't come home? You'll have to get a job."

Dick began pacing restlessly. "I suppose I should go back to school. Make it up during the summer vacation."

"How are you going to pay back from school? Daddy isn't going to help you this time. And you're not going to leave me here alone! I'm too young. I can't live alone! How'm I supposed to live?"

Dick closed his eyes. "Why don't you go clean up?"

"I'm not old enough to work! I can't make enough money to pay the rent. What are you going to do about me?"

He opened his eyes wide suddenly. "Where were you really last night?"

I stared right back. "If you don't ask me, I won't ask you—about anything!"

"Hm, hm," he shook his head.

"I'm all right! I honestly am. I wouldn't fool you about that. I'm really okay."

He stared at me some more. Sort of blankly. I think

he was beginning to feel all these problems close in on him. Missing parents, food, rent—me.

"What about the draft?" I cried. "If you're taking care of me maybe they'll give you a hardship deferment."

"Go take a shower," he said, looking off. I finally realized that he wanted to be alone and sort things out. I got halfway down the hall when he was nice enough to call after me, "And don't worry!"

I ripped off my dress and then looked at it a minute, remembering where it had been. I held it close, longing for Scorpio, even with a crazy, wild notion that if I could get him to move in with us, maybe we could all work things out. But Dick would never approve. In fact, I'd better stop thinking about Scorpio right away. At least near Dick. I shoved the dress way down in the hamper and turned on the shower.

While I was washing my hair, I heard the record player start. He was playing *Revolver,* one of his old favorite albums. Then, just as I started to rinse, I heard "Happy Days Are Here Again." The water was sort of noisy, and so I didn't really believe it. I poked my head out from the curtain and turned off the water, but there was no mistake. I almost yelled at him to turn it off, but remembered that it was part of his memories, too. And he had a lot on his mind. He had now *seen* the situation, and was probably struggling with it. Maybe he needed to go back like that, too. Like I had yesterday. He played it over and over.

While I was drying I heard him open the refrigerator door and then go away again. I realized he must be hungry. So right after I got wrapped in a robe, I padded around in the kitchen and fixed us sandwiches, and brought out some cold two-day-old chicken and took the whole tray into the living room.

Just as I'd thought, he'd looked in the refrigerator and that's all. Unless something was staring him in the face and practically saying, "Grab me!" he never fixed anything for himself. When I was little I used to think Dick actually fed himself by just opening the door and *looking* into the refrigerator.

So it was almost pathetic, really, the grateful look he gave me when I put down the tray. *On the rug.* This was something we were never supposed to do, eat on the floor. And the Chinese rug had always been so inviting that we'd always wanted to do it. Have a sort of picnic down there among the flowers with the blue butterfly.

It was such a great gesture of mine, even if I do say so! There was "Happy Days Are Here Again" playing, and here were we in our horrible independence, eating on the floor on the Chinese rug!

Sixteen

Sometimes doing a forbidden thing can affect you strangely. Even such an innocent thing as eating cozily down on a rug. No one was there to know we were doing it; we hadn't talked anyone into it; it was such a small thing that it assumed enormous proportions. I hadn't finished half a sandwich when I had another inspiration: a sort of grotesque one. I went all over the apartment drawing down all the blinds and curtains until it was good and dark. It was only around noon. Then I got candles from our emergency box and put them all around on little saucers. I brought out a framed picture of mother, and set candles on either side of it on a table.

Dick thought I was crazy. I guess I could have been sort of crazy. I was terribly tired. I was saying, "She's not coming back, so let's finish it! Let's have a wake!" On second thought, I went to get a picture of my father, too.

I don't know how or why we got into this thing, but we did. Dick even got into the mood finally. It wasn't just mother's absence; it was father's too, and the whole thing crumbling around us in this crazy way. Leaving us—US!—in this fantastic reversed position.

We dragged out all their old picture albums and started going through them from the beginning, say-

ing "good-bye." My idea. But Dick, having just returned, seemed to need something like this, too. The
only missing item was mother's small blue-bordered
card, now swinging along in somebody's pocket out
there in Tottenville. But Dick didn't know that, and
I tried to forget it for fear I might inadvertently mention it.

We found an LP album of old songs like "You're
the Top" and "Why Was I Born" and played it all—
particularly Helen Morgan singing that last one,
over and over. We sat cross-legged, eating chicken by
candlelight, listening, and looking at mother and daddy's photographs. There was Grandma Westerley and
Drew, together in front of an old '20's touring car, just
before mother was born. Grandma was obviously "big
with child," and had a happy smile.

Just think! Mother didn't even know she was going
to be born! She just *wasn't* yet! Then chubby baby
Wanda bouncing in an old-fashioned wicker carriage
with diapers on and that's all. The photo was yel-
lowed. Lots and lots of pictures of mother and daddy
as small children peeking out of various old Chryslers
and Packards. They had more cars! There was our
other grandfather, Overbrook the Second, in a straw
boater and bow tie and Palm Beach suit, grinning by
the seashore. It said Atlantic City. His wife, our Grandmother Edith, looking very chic in '20's pajamas beside him. And daddy, aged five, sitting on a pony in a
zoo. Wanda in middy blouse surrounded by dolls on
her Virginia lawn. She had an amazing number of
dolls! We went back and forth between the albums,
watching our parents grow up. It was weird. And
sort of strange that we'd never been interested before.
I noticed for the first time, even though I'd glanced
at these pictures before, that everything looked so

expensive in both families. These children just oozed good living. The quality of the clothes, the relaxed attitude of the parents, the manicured gardens, with sometimes a gardener or nurse standing around in the background. The grown-ups never seemed to be working at anything, and they all looked so clean and contented. They wore an awful lot of white, and the men seemed to really like bow ties.

"You and the Night and the Music" brought us to the '30's, and things began to change in the pictures. Got scruffier. Like the grass seemed longer. I missed the nurses and gardeners, and the carefree whoopee expressions on my grandparents' faces. Here was a picture of Wanda at her grammar school graduation, plump, not too pretty, and not nearly as well-dressed. Then Brook, looking fierce, crouched over on a football field about age twelve, and the boys in the background didn't seem the same types as before. Then the pictures began to thin out. I knew this was after the depression, and maybe they didn't take as many pictures in the depression.

There were a few school pictures—public school now, obviously, instead of their former private schools. We could tell by the look of the class and the lack of middy blouses and uniform. A shot of Grandma Westerley in her "office" at the newspaper; a dreary photo of grandpa in his wheelchair, a picture of daddy's parents just before they died. (Within a week of each other while he was at that first year of college.) I suddenly wondered what had happened to that gorgeous home of theirs outside of Philadelphia? I knew the Westerleys had lost their Virginia "mansion" after the crash, but daddy never said much about his house. And he'd left college after that first year. Why? No money to continue? Was that why he'd joined the

Army even though he didn't have to, being a Quaker? Why hadn't I ever asked him all this? I almost asked Dick if he knew, but I didn't want to spoil our silent wake and reverie.

By the time we were up to World War Two, having looked at all this through "Cheek to Cheek" and "The Lady in Red," we were both in a very strange state. For one thing, those old songs do peculiar things to you. For another, our parents, through the pictures, were becoming people and that was pretty depressing. I mean, all the security was going, going, even more than it already had for me with my thoughts about mother. Now daddy was included, too. I don't know how it affected Dick, but it conjured up all sorts of images for me.

Such as Brook and Wanda, *real children* in the really real world, before I was even around! All sorts of events that I hadn't been part of. Dolls, parties, trips —love affairs! Their marriage, for example. We eventually got to their wedding pictures which turned out to be just little snapshots. A far cry from those large, elegant, five- and six-year-old birthday party pictures. But before they got married they had to *meet!* And for all that time they hadn't even known each other!

To me that was unbelievable. I felt that my whole life was so prearranged, so predestined, that anything else—anything else that might have happened—was unthinkable! But here were all these pictures of so many different things happening to each of them in their separate lives, in separate places, that it was obvious *anything* could have happened along the way. It made me feel very insecure. Suppose they *hadn't* bumped into each other in that Washington art gallery?

I looked up from the snapshot of them emerging

from the Lutheran Church where they'd been married. Why *Lutheran,* when he was Quaker and she was Unity or Hindu or something? Or was that just another thing like Dick's baptism, because they were in a hurry? I looked up and said, "Let's get high."

He was changing the record to "Lambeth Walk" and looked at me suspiciously.

"Not grass—liquor!"

I don't think he would have liked it if I'd been smoking. See how crazy things are? It was perfectly all right for him to smoke, but not me, oh dear no!

"Booze!" I said, and before he could complain, opened the cabinet and snooped around among Brook's bottles.

"You don't drink," said Dick unsurely.

"I sure do!"

"Since when?"

I started to giggle, but didn't tell him it was just over the past three days. It did strike me that I was getting pretty good at it, though. I had hardly any hangover today. I couldn't find my drink, cognac, so I pulled out a bottle of scotch—Brook's best—and poured us some stiff ones. I believe Dick felt he should say no, but wanted a drink himself, and found this the line of least resistance. We clinked glasses and "peaced" each other.

Other than that toast, we were acting around forty years old ourselves. We were strange, anyway. It was *all* very strange! We finished up daddy's scotch along with the albums while listening to every old song, saying good-bye to Wanda and Brook by candlelight at noon.

If anyone, any stranger, or anybody, had happened to walk into our apartment and found us there like that, doing all this, I honestly believe they'd have carted us off to a psychiatric ward!

Consider what followed.

In spite of the booze, by the time we finished those albums we were feeling so peculiar that we didn't want to go on. I mean on to our *own* baby albums. By this time we felt *we* hardly existed. But we couldn't quite leave it at that, either. Something more was needed. What do you do when you're way back in time, caught in other people's lives? We were back in the '40's, unwilling to go on to the '50's and '60's, but we had to clean it all up somehow. So we dug into the record cabinet again, and unearthed our *grand-parents'* antique records—the kind that break—which mother had carefully put away wrapped in towels. And there were some doozies!

We got *way* back into the 20's, and didn't want to leave! Dick was going to say "peace" again, as we clinked, but I said "No."

"What did they say back then?" I asked.

"Cheers?"

"Okay, cheers!"

"No. Here's how!"

"Here's how!" I giggled.

"Here's mud in your eye!"

"Bottoms up!" I squealed.

Eddie Cantor was singing "Hungry Women," and we Charlestoned on the rug, and bounced around in a nutty "black bottom," and "whoopeed" and got ourselves completely out of the depression, and had a ball pretending we were back in one of those old speak-easies. The music was great. We really got into the spirit of it, and it all seemed so much more *natural!* There's something about the '20's that's sort of like the '60's and '70's somehow.

My point being that all this was actually an excellent thing to do. We were both exhausted, this exhausted us even more; it went on all afternoon (midnight to us, thanks to my lighting arrangement), so we both fell apart very early, around 7 P.M. And disappeared in a giddy, vague way, to our respective bedrooms.

Leaving scattered chicken bones, old sandwich crusts, glasses, and a generally terrible mess in the living room. I guess all the candles just burned down. We slept like logs, which was just as well. Nobody woke up to panic in the middle of the night.

We didn't know that we were really and truly alone until the next morning. Brook had not come home.

And that was when I discovered that the whole "wake" hadn't been a wake at all. What it really was, for us both, was a great big, archaic, superstitious ceremony to placate the gods in hopes that this wouldn't happen. To make it turn out so we'd get up in the morning and everybody would be there. It didn't work. It didn't bring back Wanda or Brook, mother or father, or whatever you want to call them by this time.

Dick told me the next morning, sleepy-eyed and nervous, "Jane, I honestly don't know what to do."

I had only two dollars; he had only twenty-five cents, and we had eaten up everything in the house. So, my brother went around the corner and talked himself into a little job at the garage with a little advance so we could go shopping for food and not starve.

See? In a small way, he did know what to do!

Seventeen

All the same it had happened. Remember my vision of the whole world crumbling, all the parents splitting? Here we were, right in the middle of that big possibility. But it hadn't taken place in quite the all-at-once way I had envisioned. This had been in spurts. First Dick drifted off, then mother fled deliberately, I was absent by chance, and daddy went in anger. And it didn't leave us quite the way I had foreseen, off somewhere, with nothing to come back to. Quite the opposite.

Here we found *ourselves* back at home and stuck with what was left! Maybe forever!

The apartment, the telephone, the light and gas, the problem of eating, clothes, laundry, car fare. If we'd been away and discovered long distance that our parents had split, maybe it wouldn't have bothered us. We could have ignored it, adjusted, looked off at the mountains, been happy hoboes or barefoot saints in the free generation. But being there, with everything around us, it wasn't so easy. I mean, it's hard to say, "Oh forget it," and walk out on furniture, rugs, paintings, bicycles.

As I cleared up while Dick was at the garage, I saw the place was stuffed with necessities. The TV, the hi-fi, the *albums,* records, books, clothes; I couldn't see anything that didn't look like a necessity.

My father always said how he hated possessions, and now I could see why! My mother said that deep down she disliked them, too, but with children, one had to create a home. All this wasn't only attractive; it was useful.

Now if we'd been living in the South during the Civil War and the Yankees had come through and burned everything up, that would have been different. Or if we'd been anti-Nazis in Europe and everything had been smashed or confiscated by storm troopers, that would have been different. If a bomb had fallen! Even the depression, being forced to sell for survival. But being here, *now,* even thinking these thoughts, made me fiercely possessive toward all these possessions that I actually resented.

It was crazy! I couldn't walk out on it, and neither could Dick. But what could we do? How could we maintain it? Should I try to get a job? But how much could I earn, and doing what? I hadn't even finished school and was no more trained for anything than Dick was. How had those kids up in Vermont had enough sense to get started so early! It made me mad. Why didn't I know anything? Even between us, with full-time low-level jobs doing anything, I didn't think we could earn enough to pay for all this.

And if I did get a full-time job—baby-sitting maybe?—I'd not only have to work all day, but take care of all the housekeeping, too. How could I do it? All mother's work? How did *she* do it? Of course she worked part-time, but when you put managing a whole family next to that, it worked out the same. How did they *all* do it? Work and maintain a home at the same time? Was that going to be my future? Becoming a slave to my home? Was I going to turn into my own mother? Did this sort of thing go on forever and ever? When did you ever get a day off? You didn't! Mother's days off were spent working around the house or sewing or gardening or doing all those things she never otherwise had time to do. Ohhhhhh!

If God was playing jokes or trying to lengthen my life span, he sure succeeded. That period of time I lived through was infinitely long! Every five minutes stretched to eternity. I know, because I looked at the clock, and was horrified to see that only five minutes had passed when it should have been several hours.

How did Scorpio manage to absent himself from wherever he was from so freely? Wasn't he ever torn like this? Maybe he'd think we were silly for not just walking out that very day and leaving everything just as it was. But what would happen as time went on and none of the bills were paid? Would the city come and take it all away? I couldn't bear the thought!

I should go out to Tottenville *today* with all our birth dates and times, and ask him about the *future*. He hadn't said anything about that except that I could answer my own questions about mother. But he must have been wrong, because the questions just kept piling up.

What about her? How could she walk off with just the clothes on her back, after all the blood, sweat, and tears that had gone into creating this home? If I couldn't do it, if I were too weak, how could she? Where'd she get the courage?

Another ten-year five minutes had passed. Where was my nice old, ordinary time that slipped away so quickly? Was I doomed to live like this forever? I'd be the oldest person in the world! Millions of years old! I was already exhausted.

I was at the front window, dusting around the

plants and picking up dead leaves, and thinking about the future—I had to know the *future*—when I heard a loud "beep-beep" and along came the little Road Runner kid. He zoomed along the sidewalk, arms at his side, hands straight out. I suddenly stopped. There was something in the way he moved that caught my attention. He banked around a plane tree and then whizzed off in precise half circles and curleycues, so fast that his feet looked like wheels, just like in the cartoons.

And I was suddenly transported back to that time in the gardens on Lighthouse Hill. It was so fast that I didn't even catch the transition. One second I was in that grinding anxiety about the future, the next in that other time where anxiety couldn't exist because time itself was so full. I was *there*. Seeing things, the world, the street, Road Runner.

It was such a relief! As if I'd suddenly dropped five tons of groceries! I didn't want to move. I stood there unburdened and breathing. He reappeared going in the other direction, and I shifted back into my more ordinary feeling of time.

Why did this little kid produce this change? Maybe because all children live in the present; and I needed to see him just then, so completely *in* what he was doing.

I finished cleaning the house, and the worrying didn't stop completely, but it was there with everything else I was doing in a normal way, like background musical accompaniment. I really did a good job with the place, went shopping, came back, and had everything put away plus dinner in the oven when Dick came home.

He didn't say one word about the beautiful job I'd done with the apartment. He looked hot, tired, greasy, partly proud and partly disgusted with himself. I knew he'd never worked because he *had* to before, so I tried to feel sympathetic and swallow my irritation that he hadn't said, "Oh, beautiful! Wow, what a job!" and so forth. He took a shower and we sat down to eat dinner by the window in the kitchen.

"Why aren't we eating outside?" he asked me first.

"I couldn't get around to doing the garden." It was a reasonable question because it was very nice to eat outside in the summer, and I had thought of it, but the house had taken so long.

He looked down at his plate of franks and bean casserole. "Why didn't you get a pizza?"

"You didn't say you wanted pizza!" He hadn't mentioned one word!

"You know I like pizza," he speared a frank disgustedly.

"You like franks, too," I said with a little irritation.

"I like pizza better. With Coke."

"But a pizza's more expensive than franks. We have to save money." Actually, this hadn't occurred to me before. I mean, when I was shopping.

"You had ten dollars," he growled at me.

"How did the job go today?" I said brightly, trying to be patient.

"What did you do with the ten dollars?"

"I shopped!"

"How much is left?"

"Let me eat, and then I'll look."

"I want to know now."

"I want to *eat* now!" I was getting mad.

"Who's paying for the food?"

"Oh! You're not going to get into that!" I jumped up angrily. He was acting like the "big man" and taking a real delight in it.

"How much is left?"

I wanted to pour the casserole over his head. It took a real effort to remember that he had actually worked for five whole hours in a greasy garage, that he had "tried," that those lily-white hands were in a different state than they'd ever been before. I clamped my mouth shut and got my coin purse from the sideboard. "Three dollars and sixty-one cents."

"You spent over six dollars?"

"We were out of everything!" I declared hotly. "You want a list of what I got? Want an *accounting?* Milk, bread, soup, bananas, butter, cake, soap, toilet paper, beans, franks, tomato sauce, applesauce, cereal, light bulbs—"

"What'd you get light bulbs for? We don't need light bulbs!"

"What are we supposed to see by?"

"Candles! Unless you used them all up last night!"

"You're being silly! Mean and silly! You're just dragging out everything you can think of because you want to be unpleasant—and because you hate me because now you have to take care of me," I yelled.

And the background to this were all those underneath thoughts (how do they manage to run so simultaneously?): did all men hate all women because women were dependent? And if so, why did they hate them equally much when they became *independent?* If not more so? And also, was it *always* going to be like this? He'd come home negative and hating me every night, because he'd sweated and slaved, and I'd be negative and hate him because *I'd* sweated and slaved. And he'd hate himself as much as he hated me, because he'd fallen into the trap of being responsible for me. And I'd hate myself equally because I didn't *want* him to be responsible for me, and I'd fallen into the trap of letting him be. And we'd yell at each other, or bicker, bicker, and gradually get into that trap of enjoying the bickering and yelling. And act like horrible old people who'd lived together too many years only because they *had* to. Oh, dandy! Just grand! We'd be a real normal odd couple. This whole vision got me so upset. There *had* to be another way.

I think we would have gone into a rip-roaring fight then and there if it hadn't been for this wild thing that flashed in front of me.

Dick and Jane Grow Up

I could see the title, see the book. "Here is Dick. Look at Dick worry. See Jane? Jane is angry. Look at Jane yell . . ."

And instead of yelling more, I suddenly got the giggles.

"See Dick work?" I said to my brother. "Dick has dirty hands. Look at Dick's dirty hands!"

He couldn't help smiling.

"Jane is big!" I went on, sitting down again. "Jane cleans house. Look at Jane cook. Look at Dick eat."

My brother does have a sense of humor, and he couldn't resist this. "Dick and Jane are all alone," he chanted, getting into it with me. "Father has left. Mother has left."

"Father went far away," I said, turning an imaginary page. "Mother went *very* far away!"

"See father go?" he choked, he was laughing so hard. "Look at father run. Run, father, run!"

"Mother runs faster than father and—f—farther!" I exploded. "Mother can *fly!* Look at mother! Fly, mother, fly!"

That's how we got through the rest of that day, in spite of the fact that I think we were both literally scared to death! When the doorbell rang later we stopped short. Who could be at the door? Neither one of *them* would ring. I think we had visions of more cops with—well, we couldn't imagine what, but something unpleasant. We were both very tense and giggly with the Dick and Jane game and felt so isolated, that the bell was a shattering intrusion. It really sobered us.

Dick gingerly opened the door, forgetting to look first, and there was the Western Union man. Dick signed, took the wire, started to close the door, noticed the man looked peeved, remembered he'd forgotten to tip, fished around for change, and probably gave him too much from the grocery change I'd handed over. It's simply fantastic the way money goes!

Anyway, he held the wire out to me although it was to both of us, and I backed off. "You open it."

It was from the running father who'd sent it from Pittsburgh—of all places! *May return sometime tomorrow. Father.*

Wow! It was a belated imitation of Wanda! No "Daddy," no "Love." Nothing.

"Did you ever hear of anybody who dropped out to *Pittsburgh?*" I asked my brother.

He shook his head numbly, but I noticed he was holding that wire as if it were cash in hand. He looked that relieved. I felt as if a weight had dropped, too, but neither of us wanted to come out and say so. Our pride was involved. That's probably why we talked about Pittsburgh instead.

"Who does he know in Pittsburgh?" Dick mused.

"Maybe he has a girl friend in Pittsburgh," I quipped.

"Oh, come on, Jane!"

"Why not?" I wasn't really serious, but it's interesting to note that this idea would never have occurred to me if we hadn't gone through those albums. I was still in the grip of all these "other" possibilities in our parents' lives.

Then I was struck by the word "may" in his wire. *May return*, not *will return*. What was he doing, anyway? Trying to keep us here so *he'd* have something to come back to?

"It's a plot!" I suddenly shouted. "What they're both doing is trying to turn us into their parents!"

Dick stared at me as if I were nutty. "What in the world are you talking about?"

Oh, it was too complicated to explain. But I really began to feel that the wire was out of order. I mean, after taking off like that, shouldn't he either stay away or just pop in when he felt like it? I mean, the way our family was going, any communication seemed almost improper!

Of course it was a relief, but on the other hand, it wasn't. Something had gone when the wire came—the challenge! Now the whole apartment looked different again. We looked different to each other. And I know this is crazy, but in a way it was even a disappointment. How would you feel, knowing you were on your own, making all those plans, setting your teeth for it, and then finding out it wasn't so after all? Except that you couldn't even be sure of that because your father had to go and say, "May!"

You'd think I might be used to upsets by now, but I wasn't. *I had lived a hundred years that day!*

I stared at Dick, who looked as if some angel had just flicked the planet off his shoulders. It was no good talking to him. I mumbled good night and stalked down the hall to my room, feeling stranger with each step.

Okay! He *might* return tomorrow. Well, I just *might*

be here. Or maybe I *mightn't!* I *might* just go right out to Tottenville and find Scorpio!

Might, might, might! Mother was another might. She might do this, she might do that, she might stay or go. She might hover around like ectoplasm forever!

I shut my door and flung myself across the bed, staring down at my purple shaggy rug. Every little tuft winked brightly up at me, reminding me of my terrific cleaning job. I'd even done my own room! Who was being responsible now? Them or us? Was all this dropping-out a proper way for MLU's to behave?

If I sneaked out of the house right now, avoiding Dick, how long would it take to get to Tottenville? And back? It was pretty essential to come back, because I would never be able to forget what the police had said about "a person in need of supervision." And suppose *he* returned as he *might,* and I wasn't here? Oh, this was horrible! It was like being under a huge invisible thumb. Did other people live like this? How could they do it, on the edge of disaster every single minute!

It was a long trip to Tottenville. It could take as little as four hours, or six altogether, depending on the connections. Not even counting time spent there. And money—I didn't even have any. Doomed! I threw a pillow at the wall.

I thought I'd never, not even with Scorpio, had so many thoughts or been through so many changes of feeling in one day. The thing that really bothered me was this funny deep-down reaction, under the anger and relief, of disappointment. Of something missing. I could understand the anger and relief, but I couldn't understand this additional sense of disappointment in knowing that at least one member of the Distressing Drop-Out Duo was *probably* on his way home. What was missing? How could I feel disappointed?

To say the challenge was missing was almost too easy. What did I mean by challenge? Since I couldn't go to Tottenville, was doomed to stay in, and didn't want to talk to Dick, I really chewed over this. Finally it came to me that in a way we'd lost our chance to recover the old Wild West for ourselves! Remember those pioneer days when adults could be eaten by bears or felled by crashing trees, and the kids were left to fend for themselves? And *did*? And there were no authorities around to tell them they weren't capable?

Well, that was it, the quality of it. We'd had our few shining hours right in the middle of New York City. We'd coped with the old Wild West. Even if it was mostly psychological. Even if it was in the form of rent, light, telephone, instead of blizzards and wolves. And then the chance had been taken from us before we could even face up to a *real* test. That was it! We'd only gone a little way into the experience before it was snatched away again. Maybe. Of course if he didn't come home, we'd be right back there again.

I rolled over on my back and stared at the ceiling. Suffering could be like candy, I considered. Once you started, you wanted to finish it all.

What else could I suffer over? I blinked around the room, stuffed with self-pity, and realized that the minutes were crawling along as slowly as ever. That reminded me of time, and all the various times I'd lived through. I couldn't help seeing it all unroll like a slow-motion movie; the guy with the record player and the old song down in Battery Park, the train ride, Scorpio and World War Two, Colonial Richmond-town, our wake. Even that strange experience of now time. It made me feel disoriented, like I was some infinitely ancient time taster, in the middle of an infinitely ancient universe.

There's something I sometimes do when I feel weird like this. I try to see how small I am. Sometimes it makes me feel really awful, other times it's like a liberation. The way I felt right now, I figured it should take care of all the suffering I was after in one fell swoop. I closed my eyes and imagined the universe, all the galaxies, and little old Earth, out at the tail end of one spiral. I visualized all the continents, and North America, and little old me on one dot of the eastern seaboard. And of course I was invisible. I was just like one of those minnows you never see in ponds all over the world. My room—even New York City—was just like the fish pond, and I was this wee invisible creature with teeny little arms and legs like feelers. I didn't matter at all!

This was supposed to bring more floods of self-pity, but something went wrong. I guess I was just dizzy after the whole crazy, difficult day. Because instead of suffering, or even feeling liberated, I started to have all these new questions and couldn't turn them off. Like it occurred to me that the minnow *is* really there, and it must sense where it is, all right, just like me. And I suddenly wondered if a fish feels his water like we feel our air, because they're both solid environments. But I guess it takes us to "know" his water for the fish. So who, or what, might know something like that for us? Was there lots more about the fish we really could know? Shouldn't we pay more attention?

And wasn't it fantastic that such a small, insignificant creature as myself, could even have such thoughts?

Then, right out of the blue, I remembered something. Some scientist had calculated that men were exactly halfway in size between the largest and smallest known material in the universe. Did that mean that I wasn't so small or invisible, after all?

I got even dizzier as all these thoughts spun around. And I wondered if there was some meaning here, something I was supposed to understand? Meaning and understanding, two really overworked words! Yet wasn't that what everyone was after? My mother. What else had she possibly gone off for? And my father, going from what to what? And Dick and Scorpio and me, always thinking about running away. It had to be some crazy, kooky search for meaning, from all these little "invisible" creatures. What's more, it was getting to be universal. Or at least planetary. Billions upon billions of minnows trying to jump out of their ponds . . .

Was anything better there than here? Suppose we all exchanged ponds? Then what?

I was exhausted! If there was anything I was supposed to put together from all this, any universal connection or solution, it was beyond me. My eyes were closing, and I was vibrating all over with too many cosmic questions.

I curled up without even undressing and pulled the bedspread over me. Just before I dropped off I thought three fishpond things. "Got to see Scorpio, he'll understand. Daddy probably will come back tomorrow. Wanda, please come home."

Eighteen

For the next few days I tried not to think about mother's letter and what it might mean. But it was always there, crunching with every step I took. My "theories" about time, space, and eternity, and being everywhere at once, didn't help at all. In fact it made it worse. I'd gone through all the big aches and pains and fears and now I missed her in a plain way, and all over.

What made it particularly rough was a change in our situation. It seemed that at least one of our parents was no longer an MLU. My father did come home, on the day he said he might, swinging in with his Brooks Brothers suit as if nothing had happened. But oh, had it happened, and turned everything topsy-turvy, and completely rearranged our lives! He had a new gleam in his eye, a tight mouth, and was short-tempered, firm, almost patronizing to us. He talked to us as if we were babies! We could have been right out of another Dick and Jane book—maybe *Problems Wherever We Are!* Really, it was very like that.

"Hi, Daddy. You did come home."

"Yes, Jane. I have been in Pittsburgh."

"What for, Daddy?"

"To get a new job, Jane."

"A new job, Daddy?"

"Yes, Jane. I work in the daytime now. I work for a fund-raising organization."

"What is that, Daddy?"

"It is a good thing. It gets money for people who need it."

"Why do they need money, Daddy?"

"To help them study, Jane. To go to school. It is for an educational foundation."

"I am glad, Daddy. Maybe you can help Dick. He wants to go back to school!"

New Chapter! *Dick and Daddy.*

"Dick does not want to go to school," said Daddy.

"Oh, yes, I do, Daddy!" said Dick. "I want to go right now."

"You can not go to school, Dick," said Daddy. "You must stay here and make money."

"Why must I make money, Daddy?" said Dick.

"Because you owe money," said Daddy. "I will not help you. I will not help you one bit!"

"Oh," said Dick. "Oh, Daddy!"

"One, two, three," said Daddy. "You must work!"

Next chapter! *Poor Jane.*

Daddy said, "You must work, too, Jane. You must cook. You must clean. You must care for us."

Jane said, "No, no, Daddy. I will not do that!"

"One, two, three," said Daddy. "Yes you will!"

"Oh," said Jane. "Oh, Daddy!"

But protesting didn't get me anywhere. Begging didn't work for Dick. He really wanted to go back for the summer session at his prep school, to make up what he'd missed. He didn't say anything, but I gathered that he was disillusioned with the grass scene. And he figured going back to school and studying was better than slaving in the garage. But father was ada-

mant! He wouldn't help Dick "one bit!" So my brother had to keep working in order to pay off his debt.

We were both scared about something else that
was just now beginning to be apparent. We hadn't
thought of it before. If mother did not return, and
did not go back to work, where would we get
the money for our private school tuition? This was a
real sword hanging over our heads. Dick's even more
than mine. Because he was in his senior year. *Public*
school? *For us?* Boy, was this a sobering thought.

I, for one, couldn't imagine coping with a great
big impersonal institution where you were really on
your own. I mean, what did you do without all those
extra-terribly-concerned teachers and all those marvelous parent-teacher-student conferences where you
got everything straightened out? By that I mean that
every single problem was always taken care of. By
that I mean . . . Oh, let's face it! What I really mean
is in private school you could always get things to
come out the way you wanted them to. I didn't know
whether this was possible in public school. I was fear-
ful that maybe the teachers and principals and guid-
ance counselors and psychologists were on to all the
kids, and it wouldn't be so easy. Maybe they didn't talk
things out enough to manage to confuse each other as
well as the parents. Maybe I'd be stuck!

In private school, you see, they always came to *me*
at the end of all this confusion, and wound up taking
my advice. "Well, this is what Jane feels—this is what
Jane wants." In public school I might have to do what
they wanted!

We didn't dare say a word to father about this
school thing because he was being so tough. We assumed that of course he wouldn't have enough money
to send us to private schools, although we had no way

of knowing if he was making more or less on his new job.

It was a good job; he was publicity director for this fund-raising department in an educational foundation. It turned out that one reason he had been so maniacally angry when I stayed out all night, was that I'd caused him to miss his plane to Pittsburgh. The national headquarters was there, with branch offices in New York. But he had to go to Pittsburgh to be interviewed, and he thought that being late for that first appointment might have caused him to lose out on the job. Actually, he had been planning to take me with him. So I missed a trip to Pittsburgh. Big deal!

He went into this new position with such determination and energy that you'd think he'd been waiting for it all his life. I saw what was going on instantly. What could possibly cause him to seek "regular" employment like this? What could make him give up his "project lunches" on his American Express card? His pâté and frogs legs? What could make him join the solid, brief-cased establishment?

Well, my own personal theory was that this uncharacteristic action of his was exactly like our wake! It was a great big, archaic, cultural, superstitious ceremony to placate the gods and have his wife returned to him. He obviously wasn't so happy without her. It takes two to make *real* MLU's!

And he wasn't even half an MLU any longer. We had an old-style Vermonter on our hands!

Did I ever think it might be easier to have a monster-parent like that around? Forget it! The "missing sunshine" now applied equally to father. Where were our old understanding talks? Where, oh where, was the daddy I could bend any way I wanted, like those

little rubber cartoon characters kids are always playing with? Gone! Gone with the wind that had blown
him to Pittsburgh!

His constant expression was like Mount Rushmore.
Never would a kind word cross those lips! Never again
could I appeal to his sense of "fair play." Gone were
the moments when I could appeal to him instead of
mother, and all those glorious opportunities of using
one parent against the other! We suddenly had a Captain Bligh who turned Dick into a greaser and me into a child slave.

What else? What else would you expect? What else
is a woman's role in this life? Picture me in ankle
irons, shackles, and chains. See me bending over
the tub, the sink, the floors, armed with cleansers,
brushes, rags, brooms. Watch me make beds, dust,
vacuum, straighten up, clean, clean, clean, go to the
store, go to the laundromat, and totter home with
tons of laundry and groceries.

Ever noticed how men never carry a thing? Ever
seen how free and unburdened they are? Watch and
you'll see that the most they ever carry is a newspaper,
or a skinny briefcase. Then look at the women struggling around at all hours of the day or night with paper bags, shopping carts, laundry bags, strollers, babies—and *purses!* They can't get everything into
pockets. In fact, they don't even make pockets for
women! Oh dear no, no pockets! They *deliberately*
don't make pockets, you see, just so we can get ac-
customed to carrying things. Right off! Right from
the beginning.

They start us out with pretty little purses. Then
we advance to bigger and better ones, until we finally
wind up with huge, gargantuan things that weigh a
ton! And finally graduate to still more bags. Laundry

bags. Grocery bags. And every single one of these bags corresponds to all the additional responsibilities women have!

What does a man carry in that sleek little briefcase? Nothing. A few papers *that his secretary has typed for him!*

What do women carry in their purses? Everything! Make-up. To impress men. Extra shoes. Why? For comfort? No. They don't even make comfortable shoes for women. All the comfy shoes go to men, who don't even have to *carry* anything while they're wearing them!

It's a plot! A plot, plot, plot to get us used to being uncomfortable. To toughen us up so we can *continue to carry things* under all circumstances, including burning feet. We don't need basic training. It's with us, from the cradle to the grave!

Women also carry books in their purses, first-aid junk, diapers, bottles, coin purses, wallets—credit cards! *Everything* comes out of them!

"Have an aspirin?" . . . "Oh, sure. I have a bottle of aspirin."

Naturally she has aspirin! Men never have it. They expect her to have it and *carry* it for them.

"Have a comb?" . . . "Oh sure, I have a comb. *And* a brush—right here!"

She's a walking drugstore, library, stationery store, beauty parlor, and bank. Notebooks, pencils, pens, breath inhalators, toothpaste, Band-Aids, disinfectant, Kleenex, needles, thread, scissors, diapers, bottles, toys, curlers, bobby pins, scarfs, hose, perfume, even camera and film and flashbulbs! To say nothing of bankbook, checkbook, identification, medical records, matches, pins, paper clips, and keys.

You know where I discovered all this? Staggering

to and from the laundry and supermarket for those two *males* I was supposed to be cooking and cleaning and generally "caring for." Taking mother's place, naturally. And I never, never, realized, until I'd gone through this, just exactly what Wanda had been doing all these years.

Oh boy, was I suddenly with her! I mean taking off for India. I was ready to take off myself. Just to get *unburdened!* Just to get my hands loose from *things.* Although I missed her terribly, I couldn't feel very sorry for myself, because I began to feel so sympathetic. It may sound crazy that the supermarket was what caused me to fall way over on *her* side, but that's literally what happened.

I'd stand there in line, loaded down with groceries, and watch the women fending off two or three children, wrestling with laundry bags, milk, potatoes and juice. They'd dig through layers of bubble gum, mail, rain hats, the drugstore—everything—to find their usually wee little coin purses stuffed way down in the bottom. The register would go click, blink, clump, and the cashier would be blithely humming while the females stared frantically at the prices going up, up, up, all the time shooing babies away with one hand while they held *things* in the other, and looked for their coin purses practically with their noses! They never had a free hand!

The ones who didn't have children, the well-dressed young secretaries, would stand there and do a funny little dance. Naturally, their *feet* hurt in those lousy shoes!

And others would have a terrible time, because they'd lose something on the floor, but didn't have any free appendages—like *hands*—to find it. Big fat curlers, for example, suddenly falling out from under

their scarfs, because they had their hair up in anticipation of an evening with a male for whom they were
carting home all this stuff. Ohhh! *Carriers of the world,
unite!*

They also always had terrible problems with logis-
tics and transportation as they went back and forth
from the laundry to the supermarket. Should they do
laundry first, or get food? How many bags of groceries
could sit comfortably on top of how many laundry
bags? Could you possibly add a *child* to all this? Like
a cherry on top. Would he perch there, or fall off?
Maybe she should put the laundry on top of the groceries? But then she'd squash the bananas and let-
tuce. Maybe she should put the *kid* in the middle, on
top of the laundry. Would he hold the groceries? Or
would she have one mashed child?

On the other hand, she could have groceries all over
the street. Besides, there was also a stroller to contend
with, at least one other child, dry cleaning, school
lunch boxes and briefcases, and heaven knows how
many other side trips to the dime store, the hardware
store. You need to be an octopus for this!

Octopuses of the world unite!

If she were really clever she could put the dry cleaning over one arm, handles of lunch boxes and briefcases over the other arm. One hand for one stroller
and one hand for the shopping cart. And the laundry
could go over her shoulder! Disaster! She'd forgotten
one child!

Maybe if she took the laundry home first, she
could leave the kids with someone? Come back? That
only created more transportation problems. Okay, no
coming back. Did she have everything? Where, in her
purse, was which list for what? Just before they left,
there was this awful, dreadful look of desperation.

Had they forgotten anything? God forbid that they ever had to come back!

And you know what else I noticed? The men always looked *the other way* when they saw these creatures! I mean, cashiers, clerks in the supermarket, the laundromat attendant. They'd never look any woman who was carrying all this junk right in the eye. They'd look off somewhere, as if it was some kind of embarrassment to them. You know why? They were guilty! The only ones they'd ever look at were the young secretaries. But the minute *she* got all bowed over with her three-ton purse, groceries, dry cleaning, parcels of clothes that she had to keep constantly buying so she'd be attractive to the men at the office—the minute she was bristling and crackling with ten dozen assorted paper bags, like a walking department store—they'd look away again!

Oh, grrrrrr! *Burden-beasts of the world, unite!*

The very least they could do was send us to the moon where things would weigh less. On second thought, no. No! That's just what they want us to think. Maybe this is all a terrible preparation for becoming interplanetary hod carriers! *They'll* go up there in their sleek little capsules, just like their briefcases. And we'll follow in two-ton space trucks! Carrying all their stuff! They'll zoom off and hop around with nothing in their hands, and we'll follow after like *squaws*, carrying *their* shovels, *their* pickaxes, *their* Mars stones. Maybe they won't even carry their own life-support system! They may be training us right now to carry *their* oxygen, *their* food, *their* communication systems—on our backs. *On top of our own!*

Astro-women of the world, unite! Before it's too late.

Well, you can see how emotional I got about all this.

And maybe you can understand how it made me feel closer and closer to Wanda. She might be my mother, but we had this other thing in common. We were both females. And I started to wonder if maybe she hadn't gone to India just to get her *hands free?*

I began to dread going out because of the *things* I had to do, the *things* I had to carry home. When I'd been going to school, carrying my books and stuff, it hadn't bothered me. Not really. Not in a big way. But this was oppressive. Because now I was doing it all for other people? And not for myself? That was part of it, but the thing that really got to me, to the bottom of my soul, was that there was *no response* to what I did, or carried, from either Dick or daddy.

Men—and I was sure that daddy and Dick were pretty symbolic of them all—never carried much of anything, and yet they acted as if they carried it all! Dick would walk in with nothing but greasy hands, but he *looked* as if he was toting the whole garage! He had invisible tires and wrenches and rags sprouting out all over him. Daddy would come in with nothing except that briefcase with maybe two sheets of paper inside. But he looked and acted as if he were weighed down with tons of the company's funds in silver dollars, plus half the public library.

I'd stare at my father, wondering when I had last seen him weighed down with anything. What did he ever carry? Oh, an occasional, *very* occasional bag for my mother. I'll grant him that. He might carry one bag, if he was around, while she carried another. But most of the time he wasn't around. And why should she carry that other bag, anyway? Why couldn't he carry them both? Wasn't he strong enough?

One night he caught me looking at him with this terrible expression. I was trying to remember my most

vivid impression of father loaded down with something. *Anything!* What did I recall ever seeing in his
hands? And this picture came—*fun* things! Sleds,
Christmas trees, picnic baskets.

I squeezed my eyes and blinked at the memory of
him loading the rented car for that trip to Vermont.
He put in the games, balls, swimming fins; while *she*
put in the suitcases, extra sweaters, all the necessities.

And I was devastated! Because I suddenly wondered
what image of their parents children can possibly
have, when daddies are always loaded down with *fun*
things, and mommies with the slavish, familiar, unex-
citing *necessities*.

He was gazing at me, concerned, "Is something the
matter, Jane?"

I couldn't answer because I was so overwhelmed
by the impression. *I* had also looked at mother like
a necessity to take care of other necessities. A carrier,
a squaw, someone there to carry supplies. You didn't
have to be a little boy; it wasn't only males. Little
girls looked at their mothers like that, too, *in spite*
of all their bringing up. In spite of MLU parents.
In spite of being told their parents were persons,
and trying hard to believe it. It didn't matter. You
couldn't get away from the inevitable *physical,* day-
to-day images of your mother and father.

And *that* was the life in store for me? That was
my destiny? Becoming another life-support system,
with never a free hand? There *must* be something better you could do with these "feelers," as I'd thought of
them. Some other way you could be that minnow in
the pond.

"What is the *matter,* Jane?" Daddy was on the
couch, and he put down his newspaper to look anxiously at me over his glasses.

What could I tell him? I had too many thoughts, extensions of thoughts, too many strange and wild new ideas. They say teenagers sometimes get sort of psychopathic. I believe it! I think I was! But I also think it came from my rather unique situation. In general it may come from all these questions involving how to best change or improve the future. I mean, ourselves, what we are and what we're going to be.

Would I, or would I not have been a candidate for the local loony bin if I had screamed, as I wanted to, "It's all insane!" Just like Scorpio had told me. I wanted to go further! I wanted to tell my father that *everything* was the matter. That I was not—repeat NOT—very anxious to become a hod carrier. My mother had walked out with her clothes and a—yes—purse, purse, purse. *I didn't ever want to even carry a purse!*

I didn't know what she was doing in India, but I hoped her hands were free, free, free!

I didn't want to have to attach a child like a cherry to the top of a shopping cart and pray he wouldn't fall off.

Imagine how this would have sounded to my father!

All this, the thoughts, impressions, the horrors, went on for four days. And it was another lifetime! And I couldn't get out of the apartment at all. I mean, to do my *own* thing. *He* would leave me all these other things to do, and call me up from time to time to see that I was about my business—woman's business—Wanda's business—and was safe, and not trying to sneak out for the night. He even put Dick on my trail, I know.

It was too much! Everything put together was enough to make you join a women's lib group!

But in all conscience, I couldn't do that, either. I

couldn't even think of anything militant for females because of the eternal, lousy Eve problem. During all of this I had Scorpio on my mind constantly!

There were these terrible physical sensations of fluttering heartbeat, elevator stomach, internal rumblings and external tremblings. And I couldn't get out to see him! At the same time, by then, I hated the whole male-female thing! I kept telling myself Scorpio was different. At least he carried his own pack on his own back. So it was okay for me to have an elevator stomach every time I thought of him.

He carried his own pack! Somewhere out there in Tottenville.

Was this the wonderful meaning of *us?* My generation? Would we learn to carry things a little more equitably, more fairly? Would our children have a better sense—a better "feel"—of who they were?

When I looked at my father I had the most overwhelming feeling of sorrow for him. He never knew what he saw in my eyes. When I thought of my mother I suddenly knew she wanted all the same things I did. Always had. So had he, my father, always.

And so did Dick, although he hadn't thought much about it yet. But he would when he met a girl and his future started to move in to him.

And then I started wondering what I could invent in order to flee from poor Captain Bligh and get out to see Scorpio.

Nineteen

Two nights later I got an inspiration. Daddy was in Dick's room, watching television. He shushed me until the commercial came on, and then I had to talk fast.

"I'd like to get a job for the summer if it's okay with you. I'll start looking for one tomorrow—if it's okay with you."

"Fine! Go ahead. They might have some summer jobs at the foundation. I'll ask for you."

"I'd really prefer to find my own job. I think finding the job is part of the whole experience."

"All right, do that. If you have any trouble, let me know." He gave me only one suspicious glance before returning to the TV. I had the impression that he *had* to say yes to this request, but wasn't too sure about it. But he wouldn't discuss it with me as he might have in the past, because of his new approach to dealing with his children. He rarely said anything any more. He tried to let us know by *looks* just what he expected. And the light in his eyes when I left the room told me that job or not I would be expected to continue doing all my other work as well.

Oh, you can't imagine how it felt—or maybe you can—to be back in my old "invisible" outfit again, crossing the harbor with the blue sky and space all around, going somewhere I really wanted to go—with nothing in my hands! Freedom! And a terrific excitement in the pit of my stomach. Would he be there?

I was so impatient on the train it was a good thing my friendly neighborhood conductor wasn't there. I kind of hoped to see him again, but not today—not today! Finally we got to Tottenville, and I tore up to the bar trying to *will* Scorpio to be inside—and naturally he wasn't.

I sat there for hours at "our table," listening to "our songs" on the juke box, "Sentimental Journey," "That Old Black Magic," "Lili Marlene"; drinking gallons of Coke, waiting, hoping. The shadows got longer and longer among the weeds outside—and he never came. I kept having to go to the ladies' room, because I'd never spend long enough inside because I'd panic that he might come in and I'd miss him. Nobody paid any attention to me, nobody tried to pick me up, and I began to wonder if I was really there.

Finally I asked Harry if he had seen "my friend." He didn't hear me right the first time, so it was embarrassing when I had to shout, *"My friend!"* Hoping he'd know who I meant.

Oh, he hadn't forgotten us! "Fella in the black boots! Sure. He was in yesterday. Think he might have been looking for you."

My stomach flopped, I was so relieved.

"I'll tell him you was here," said Harry.

I had to leave. I was going to be terribly late getting home, and I still had the shopping to do, and I had stories to think up about where I'd been to get a job.

This went on for three more days! Each day, on the way home, I'd invent lists of places I'd been to "seek employment," and was scared that my father might call one of them to see if I'd really been there. To allay suspicion, I might even have to *get* a job. But since I made it a point to get home at a reasonable time, with all the groceries and laundry and odds and ends, and since I was always so tired, he seemed to accept my stories. My big tale was about a chain of bakery stores where I'd left an application, and they did hire teenagers, and would probably be calling me soon. But in the meantime I was scouting around for something better. Even Dick believed me!

By the third day I despaired of ever seeing Scorpio again. He hadn't been in the bar at all, and never got Harry's message about me. How could I find him? How could you track someone down who floated around Staten Island with a pack on his back?

The fourth day was bleak. There was an iron-gray glare in the sky; it was hot, and there was a lot of smog and pollution. From the water you could see this terrible pall hanging over New York and New Jersey. The docks at Staten Island appeared just as you got to them, out of this gloom. I arrived at the bar in a very gray mood myself, feeling like something mechanical that was just wound up to travel back and forth to Tottenville every day for no reason at all.

And there he was! Sitting at "our table" with an air of never having left. Right away I didn't care if I got home on time—or ever got home at all!

"Hi," I said, quivering all over at seeing him again.

You might think that after not seeing him for over two weeks, he wouldn't look as good to me, or I might be disappointed, or find my dreams smashed or something. Not at all! He looked better! Handsomer. His hair was even longer—naturally. But somewhere or other he kept shaving, because his face was clean. His eyes were still beautiful and deep and mysterious and magnetic, and he seemed more like Heathcliff than ever. I was shattered! In that great, delicious way.

"Hi. Was everything all right when you got home?" he asked, just as if it had been *yesterday* when I left him!

"No, it wasn't really okay." And I told him all about the police, and my father, and Dick, and the wake, and our new situation, and the letter from mother—everything. Everything except what I really wanted to tell him, which was about all my private thoughts. But I didn't know how, so I kept babbling about all this other junk, and somehow trying to make it funny.

He said, "All this sounds like you have to be home very early. A 5 P.M. Cinderella. I don't dare even offer you a drink."

"Oh, yes you do," I said quickly. "Yes you can. This is, uh, sort of a day off. I'm free today."

"Oh, before I forget," and he pulled out mother's birth announcement from his pocket and handed it to me.

It felt strange to have it in my hands again, now that I felt differently about her. Scorpio watched me curiously as I took it and put it into my raincoat pocket. I wanted to say something about all my discoveries: about mother, life-support systems, free hands, space, time, eternity, our generation—but the words wouldn't come. Maybe I had to be drunk to talk about these things!

It was terribly quiet here, back in 1945. Harry was wiping glasses and each one he put down on the counter made a loud clink. I glanced his way and when I looked back at Scorpio I had a fast, fleeting impression of something sad and thoughtful in his expression. It changed the minute I caught his eyes.

"Okay," he smiled quickly, "cognac?"

I nodded; he rose to get our drinks and to play "That Old Black Magic," and the black bird called out, "Buy war bonds! Buy war bonds!"

Scorpio returned, plunking down our drinks, throwing his legs over the chair, as he always did. I had a premonition, however, from the look on his face.

"You're not saying good-bye, are you?"

"To what?"

"Everything! The bar, World War Two, 1945—me."

"I never say good-bye!" He grinned. "You asked me that the last time."

"But are you saying good-bye in a little way?"

"Of course not. How can I say good-bye when you and I just got here? Come on, Pisces, *salut!*"

We clinked glasses, and when he saw me down the whole shot of cognac in one gulp—I wanted to get drunk real fast so I could *talk* to him—he said, "I have a horrible feeling I'm demoralizing a minor. What's your father going to say when you come home with booze on your breath?"

"I don't care! What he says, or what Dick says—" And that reminded me that I had to tell him my real name. I wanted him to know it, so he could look me up in the phone book. Suppose something happened. How could he ever find me only knowing Pisces, Dick, Overbrook, and Wanda?

"Please may I tell you my real name now? I have a joke, and I can't tell it without telling my name." (My idea was about being Dick and Jane, which I had a feeling he would appreciate.)

"No."

"Just my first name? And I promise not to tell the

last?" That could always "slip out" later on.

"No."

"Then will you tell me your name? Who you are?"

"No."

"Not even if I beg, plead, pray, get down on the floor and grovel?"

"Nope. You know my name, anyway."

"Scorpio?"

"Yep."

"With Leo rising?"

"Right."

"But I'd rather know a *different* name!" I insisted.

He smiled. "Then call me Saturn in mid-heaven."

Saturn in mid-heaven! Something clicked. That's what he'd said about mother! So! They had some big astrological thing in common! Maybe that's why he'd acted so mysterious about her—so interested. Had they both done the same things, in different ways?

"May I have another drink?" I asked.

"No . . . yes. One more, and then I'll put you on the train before it changes into a pumpkin."

"I just got here!" I protested.

"You know, you're a leech, Pisces, a burr. Terribly difficult to get rid of." He was smiling at me and my stomach flopped again because it sounded like he meant more than he was saying.

"Don't *you* ever go home?" I prodded, still thinking about him and Wanda.

"I am home." He smiled. Then he jumped up to get my second cognac.

What did he mean by that? When I watched him pay Harry, I also wondered what he lived on, where he got his money. He didn't have an American Express card! Did his family send him an allowance? Where would they send it? How did he live? Funny that I hadn't wondered about this before. I suppose it wouldn't have occurred to me except for those two elemental days when Dick and I faced the how-to-sustain-yourself question.

I watched him return from the bar. Same black boots, same red plaid shirt, same pants—but clean! How did he manage that? Where did he bathe, shave, take care of himself? That sister he'd spoken of, was she married? Did she live here in Tottenville? Did he drop in to her house to do all these things? Or was she some psychopathic teenager like me?

He seemed to have some feeling for her, from the way he'd spoken. Why did he seem sad today? And why couldn't I talk to him, and get out my big, sad, serious thoughts?

When he came back he asked me, "If Wanda doesn't come back, Pisces, how are you going to feel?"

"I don't know." I stared at him. "I'll miss her. Do you *know* that she isn't going to come back? Did you make up her chart?"

"No." He smiled. "But I suppose it's a possibility. Just wondered how you might feel about it, You know"—he grinned suddenly—"even if she doesn't come back, it isn't as if she'd fled to Miami!"

I was bug-eyed!

"Come on, drink up and I'll take you to the train."

There was a terrible glare coming in the long window. The top of the table was hot. Even the little cognac glass felt warm when I picked it up. I wished it would rain and storm and pour all over us. I hated this hot, gray day.

"*Salut,* Pisces!" he urged, and we drank up to "Lili Marlene."

Everything was going wrong. I was still encased in all my disguise junk. He hadn't asked me to take it off. He hadn't asked me to go anywhere, to tell him anything!

He pulled me up, waved good-bye to Harry, and walked me to the door. Just as we got outside, a car drew up in front of the bar. That horrible old guy got out, that nasty creature who had tried to pick me up the first day I came here. It gave me chills. It was like another premonition. I kind of leaned against Scorpio, but he didn't seem to notice. We walked down the sidewalk, to the bottom of the hill.

There's nothing there, just across from the train station. Weeds, straggly bushes, and undergrowth, a muddy shoreline of Staten Island. Scorpio took me down to the water, through a path of sorts, over the partly muddy and partly scorched ground, strewn with litter: cigarette butts, papers, bottles, rusted cans. I thought of the Tibetan gardens. He pulled me down beside him and we sat on a piece of old piling, looking out at the oily gray water of the channel between the island and New Jersey. Off to our left a few sailboats from the yacht club were moored, rolling slowly on the thick water.

"Do you know this is where New York begins?" he said. "One of the first things Harry ever told me was that Tottenville is the true beginning of New York. Of course if you came in from the other direction, you could call it the end."

"Well," I swallowed, "Let's say you call it the beginning. Couldn't you branch out a little? Like going on to Manhattan?"

He laughed.

Suddenly I blurted out, "My real name is Jane Elizabeth Andrews and—" I gave him my address so fast he couldn't stop me. Then I was scared. What would he do?

He looked at me, rose, pulled me up, and then slowly kissed me. And although I'd dreamed and dreamed about this, I couldn't be *in* it as much as I wanted, because it felt so final. Had I ruined everything? He couldn't be saying good-bye, we were just beginning.

When he let me go, I looked at him. "You've been drafted! You're going! Is that it?"

"Of course not." He smiled, but he could have been lying.

"Then you've decided not to go. You're going to Canada instead. Is that it?"

"You know which war I'm in, Pisces. Come on, train time."

I pulled back when he took my hand. Overhead the sky was leaden. Plumes of smoke were drifting across the channel from the smokestacks in New Jersey. I stared at his 1890's long hair, his in-between clothes that didn't belong to any time, and asked something outrageous. "Are you really from back then? 1945?"

He was so astonished that he looked as if he didn't know whether to laugh or feel sorry for me. I didn't feel stupid about my question. I felt morbid, and all mixed up.

"I mean, do you sort of drift through time, in general? Or, when you go into that bar is it really 1945 and World War Two for you?"

"In a way. It's one place, anyway, where I don't feel like an objector."

Which gave me another horrible idea. "You're going to be *noble* about it! You're going to burn your draft card and wind up in jail!"

"Train time!" He grinned, refusing to respond to any of this.

We marched back to the street, through the mud

and weeds, and he tried to jolly me by singing "Jolly Sixpence." I felt it was an act. I felt something serious was about to happen with him, and he was trying to be kind or brave by not telling me. On the other hand maybe he was just concerned about getting me home on time. He was sure trying to get me off in a hurry. *Why* had I opened my big mouth and told him all about those new problems with my father?

By the time we'd walked up the ramp to the waiting train, I felt like a World War Two bride in reverse. He was seeing *me* off, and I wasn't going anywhere!

We stood by the train doors for a moment. A young conductor was waiting by the rear car for me to get on. I looked up in an agonized way. "Will I see you? Will you . . . ?"

"Sure, Pisces," he took my face in his hands and kissed me again—right in front of the conductor! "I'll see you. *Ciaou!*"

Just as I got on, he said, "We'll have to go back to Lighthouse Hill someday."

I sat down as the train started off with a jerk, and looked back at him standing underneath the shed, waving at me. I felt like bawling! It had all happened so fast! We hadn't really said anything. This entire meeting had been on an unsaid, unspoken level. Did he really mean I'd see him again? Would he be there when I came back?

I was all crouched over, teary, bleak, and miserable on that long ride to St. George. The only thing that lifted me out of it was remembering what he'd said about going back someday to the gardens on Lighthouse Hill.

Twenty

Someday when I'm an old, old lady, I'll still be able to feel the movement of that Tottenville train. The jerks and rattles will get all mixed up with the taste of cognac and the smell of the old wood in the bar, and the sound of "Lili Marlene" and the bird calling out World War Two slogans. I'll hear strains of "Happy Days Are Here Again" and "Why Was I Born" mixed with the Beatles, and the smell of daddy's scotch, franks and beans, dust on the Chinese rug—and that'll all get mixed with the whiff of Scorpio's shirt. I'll dream of him and have visions of the house in Richmondtown, and blue skies and rain pounding against the window in the bar. I'll taste blackberry brandy, Scorpio's kiss, see him climbing out the window with the pack on his back; see Harry with his sleeves rolled up in rubber bands, Road Runner zooming around the tree. And I'll see and feel the Tibetan gardens and all the strangeness of time.

I know this is going to happen, because it's happening already, every time I feel—sort of in the "seat of my pants"—the peculiar motion of that Tottenville train.

I kept going out, of course. I went back every day for several days, looking for Scorpio. It began to feel so unreal that I wondered if I was really there, or if any of this had really happened.

Every time I went into that bar, for instance, I'd make it a point to touch "our" table, and say to myself, "Now I'm in 1945!" Before I left, I'd put my hand on the old bar, "It is now 1890." I suppose it was pretty crazy, but it came from being alone on the train all the time, and not finding Scorpio, and all my questions about time tasting.

For a while I was even convinced that Santa Claus had been a figment of my imagination, and didn't exist at all—until I saw him again. He was on the train one day, and delighted to see me. But when I shook his hand I found myself thinking, "This is now the 1930's!"

He smiled at me quizzically, "Jane, my dear, you have an expression that something big is going on! Are you full of happiness or torment? Or both? Ah!"

Something in my expression must have delighted him. He glowed rounder and rosier than ever, and plunked down in the seat opposite me, full of anticipation. "Tell me about it!"

"Well—" I started. And the sound of my own voice was a real shock, I'd been riding alone on that train for so long. "Well—mother hasn't come back."

"Yes," he smiled happily, "I see."

"And, uh, my father's—different."

"Oh, yes? Stricter? More difficult? Sort of a monster these days?"

"Yes," I mumbled. He seemed so delighted about everything!

"But it's perfectly understandable! Predictable. Nothing to get excited over." He looked at me closely. "But then you're not so excited any more, are you?"

I stared into those incredible, sparkling blue eyes. "No! I'm not!"

"Just—pondering?" he asked with a lovely smile.

"Y—yes!"

"About everything?"

"Yes!" I started to cry and he pulled out a little package of Kleenex and gave me one. He actually carried something useful that didn't come out of a *purse!*

While I was sniffling he tactfully looked at his watch and chuckled, "You know, it's delightful to see you on your way home at such a reasonable hour! I can't honestly say I'm sorry daddy's being difficult."

"Oh, I've been coming home early lots of days, but I haven't seen you."

"Been out to Tottenville often?"

"Yes."

"Looking for something, Jane?"

"Yes."

"Looking for *him,* I suppose."

I blew my nose, wide-eyed. "Do you *know* him? Have you seen him? Do you know who I'm talking about?"

"Well," he looked out the window, "If you're referring to a young fellow with dark hair, handsome—quite handsome, indeed—who sometimes wears a plaid shirt—"

"Do you know his name?"

"I am sorry, my dear, but I do not. In fact, I wasn't certain that he was your young man, although I wondered—" He chuckled again. "I certainly did wonder when he followed you to the train that night."

"What night? When did he follow me?"

"When I first met you, my dear," Santa beamed. "You were a bit under the weather but struggling valiantly. Oh, you were making a noble effort!"

"And he was *there?*" I couldn't believe this! I'd

walked out alone that first night!

"Way down at the end of the station, as observant as a watchdog! He seemed quite concerned about you. He certainly didn't take his eyes away until he saw I had you safely in tow. Seemed like a nice young man, even lurking in the shadows like that. Waved at me, as a matter of fact, when I got you safely aboard."

That first night! When I'd thought he didn't even know I was drunk! When I'd thought he wouldn't even care if he did know!

"And have you seen him again?" I begged.

"Just once, he was walking up the hill from the station. Had some sort of equipment on his back. Looked as if he might be going off for a hike." He gazed into my eyes with interest. "But then I gather the hikes you young people take today are quite different . . .

"Well, my dear," he patted my hand, "I mustn't keep you. I see you have deep thoughts on your mind. I've never liked to interrupt these private sessions. They come only at certain times, as we both know."

I watched him hop to the door and stop the train just in the nick of time at the next station. Then afterwards he plopped himself down beside a young and very modern nun, one of those in the short skirts. They huddled together all the way to St. George, and of course by the time she left the train she was glowing and looked a lot less modern.

After he'd been with me, I found that my thoughts were faster and clearer and fell into place better, like a mess of tangled thread starting to unsort itself.

I was *waiting* to understand. And I saw that I always did this. I'd always expected all these gifts of understanding to come and sort of present themselves to me at appropriate intervals, like you get a bike for Christmas the year you're old enough. I guess I thought that if I lived long enough, I'd eventually understand everything! I'd be sheer living genius by the time I was one hundred!

And I realized something else. I also expected, every time one of these "understanding" packages was handed to me, all wrapped up in ribbons, that then something miraculous would immediately happen. Like *now*—I was waiting to understand it all. And then after I did, I'd immediately find Scorpio; the very next day I'd wake up and mother would be home; Daddy would return to his old style, and everything would go on exactly as it had before.

I saw, looking out the window as we approached the end of the trip, that this wasn't going to happen! Whether mother came home or not, whether I found Scorpio or not, nothing would ever be just the same. We were all different now.

Besides! Maybe we understood enough already! *Maybe everybody already understood everything!*

Why hadn't I thought of this before? In some way it even fit into my theory of being eternal. There was something the same between all of us, all these different ages. From the little Road Runner to old Harry the bartender, from Scorpio and Dick and me to my conductor—with mother and daddy somewhere in between. It was all the same; all one generation—the one that was alive.

There wasn't any such thing as a real generation gap! People were crazy to think there was any real distance between them, that they didn't understand each other.

The only possible gap could be between those who were dead and those who were alive right now. And I even wondered about that. So why was I waiting for understanding? Maybe we didn't need any more understanding. Maybe we needed to be more, do more—do more about the understanding we already had.

I *know* that this was one of those very important and perhaps true thoughts, because it made me so nervous! It really did! It kind of brought all my other ideas together, and at the same time it sort of pushed me onwards and upwards toward all sorts of other things I was going to have to think out. Like, if I really already understood what was going on there at home, and what was going on with Wanda in India— maybe I'd have to act a little different.

Worse! I wouldn't—at least if I had the courage of my own convictions about this—be able to wiggle out of anything by telling even *myself* that I didn't understand it!

I hadn't thought about cigarettes for a long time, but I carried them with me—just in case. Now I had one. The conductor noticed, but didn't say anything. At St. George he said good-bye to the nun and then walked me off the train.

"Life is not a bowl of cherries, is it Jane?"

"No." I felt embarrassed about the cigarette which I hadn't finished, and crushed it under my sneakers.

"But it's beautiful, all the same."

"I guess so—" I stood there under those grimy, gloomy train sheds, beside the wired train window, and suddenly felt I owed this man something.

"Uh—I did discover something." It was a real effort to push these words out. "There—there really isn't any real generation gap!"

"I know!" he said sympathetically. *"Terrible,* isn't it?"

I stared at him.

He put a hand on my shoulder and walked me past

the train, onto the steps of the ferry arcade. "What a day for you, Jane! What a day when one discovers that! Takes all the joy out of living for a while, I know. No more excuses, no more fun pretending one doesn't understand."

I stumbled on a step. His hand caught me firmly under my elbow. "No more jolly times blaming the older generation, or even—" We stopped at the head of the steps and he twinkled at me from under those eyebrows, "Even blaming the *younger* generation, hm? No indeed!"

He looked off down the arcade, past the hot dog stand, the bakery shop, the throngs of people hurrying by. "No, it's a dark day when one discovers that. Old or young, it makes the world explode. Puts one in one's place—a very small place, by the way. Yes indeed. Leads to all sorts of responsibilities and efforts. Tch, tch! Difficult day. I had a feeling you might be coming to that."

I was still frozen, staring at him.

"But I promise you, Jane!" his cheeks lifted up into rosy little apples, "I absolutely promise you'll enjoy it in the end! Just go ahead and suffer for awhile, my dear. It is worth it, in the end. I know."

With a pat, and a wave, he walked away. I gazed after him. *Of course he knew!* All his little remarks, "You young people," "I understand," "Difficult these days," "A nice, soothing bath, my dear," "When one has imbibed too much . . ."

When, on what day, month, what year, had he understood that he understood? And now he was involved with everybody, all generations, all ages. I knew! I'd seen him!

He waved back at me, "You'll find him eventually! I'll be crossing my fingers."

And I waved back, acknowledging him. Age sixteen waving to—how old was he?—sixty? sixty-six?

I didn't have any more cigarettes. I got on the ferry, looked at the sky, and went home.

Twenty-One

Naturally nothing turned out as I dreamed or imagined it might. There was no word from India. Mother didn't send any letter or telegram saying she'd be home. I never figured out what she meant in her last letter; I didn't look through her books to try and find out; I didn't join a Buddhist or Hindu study center to find out what I was missing. Dick did not go back to school, daddy did not "repent" and pay his bill; I did not find Scorpio, I did not take a job.

What actually happened was that one morning, a few weeks later, I smelled coffee. I got up, thinking it was daddy, and that it was our regular getting up time. Actually it turned out to be only 5:30 A.M. And it was my mother making coffee in the kitchen, which, as you'll remember, is right next to my room.

And, of course, it was all terribly reasonable. She hadn't let us know when she was coming because she wasn't sure herself; hadn't asked anyone to meet her because it was so early in the morning. And why should anyone have to meet her? She only had the clothes she'd left in, her *purse,* and one extra parcel. She'd just taken a cab from Kennedy, walked in, and started making coffee.

If you think everything went "swimmingly" after she came home, you're wrong! Daddy was furious! He seemed to have saved his anger at her until she got home. And she'd evidently never had a real intention of *not* coming home, which made all my agonies about it so ridiculous.

But I'm leaping ahead. On that early morning when I found her I groped my way out of bed and stumbled into the kitchen. Picture mother just pouring herself a cup of fresh coffee. Picture me blinking at her from my nightgown.

I said, "Hi."

She said, "Jane!" And smiled, and kissed me, and we were terribly affectionate for about two minutes. You know how it is when you're still sleepy and not awake and any human thing seems like a teddy bear. I just sort of crawled into her hug. It felt nice. It's good, really, to be affectionate with your mother once in a while.

But then I looked to see where she'd changed. She still looked the same, really, except her hair was all straight and pulled back into some hasty tail. I guess she hadn't time for anything else. No! She didn't look the same. Her circles were better. Nearly unnoticeable. She did look clear and rested. But she had the same face, same skin, same smell . . . no, again! There was a different, unusual, vaguely subtle smell about her.

I sniffed at her a bit and she gave me another big hug. "Oh, it's good to see you again!"

"Did you have a good time?" I asked *inanely*. It was too early for all this! That wasn't what I wanted to say at all!

"Want some coffee?" She grinned, with enough sense not to answer me.

No—yes—went my head, and she poured me a cup. "Imagine you being up at this hour! Jane, that's the nicest homecoming I could have had!"

I must have been closer to my true baby self than usual, because I nuzzled into her shoulder again and had to blink back some tears before I took the coffee. I gave her another kiss before I came out with all these stupid 5 A.M.-in-the-morning honest questions.

"If you didn't have a good time, what else happened?"

We walked into the living room to have our coffee. It was so early we could hear the birds chirping over in Carl Shurz Park.

"Lots!" She smiled. "And I notice Dick is home!"

"Mmm. He came back right away after you left." I gulped coffee, trying to wake myself up. "How does it feel to be home?" Another stupid, honest question, but *she* looked as if it was the kind of thing she was used to.

"I don't know yet. It feels—strange."

"What was it like?"

"It was—" she suddenly chuckled, *"not* ineffable!" That was sort of to herself. I don't believe she knew I'd overheard that particular conversation. "It was very hard. Getting up early in the morning. It was very beautiful. What I wanted. A good rest."

This was all followed by a lot of unspoken words. "I don't want to talk about it any more now. That's enough about it."

And *I understood!* I knew she couldn't really talk about it! I didn't even want her to! Could I possibly tell her what had happened to me? Where I'd been all this time? Ridiculous!

We had, at that moment, a perfect understanding!

"You look both rested and tired," I said.

"Oh, I'll be okay," she sipped coffee, looking around the room, and then at me, "How *are* you, Jane?"

"Oh, I'll be okay," I sipped coffee, looked around the room, and then at her. "I understand everything now!"

"Do you, Jane?" she replied very seriously.

And that's where I was caught up short! There was something about her just then that was incredibly, scarily, like my conductor! She *was* different! Something had changed! I wasn't a little girl any more, the way she asked that. I was some growing person—myself. Not connected so much to her, not her daughter there for her. I was a person.

Everything worked both ways in the whole world!

"You *do* understand, Jane?" She helped me out by smiling just like a mother.

"Well, some things. I know *all* about carrying things."

But did she know what I was talking about now, I wondered? "But there's one thing I wish you'd tell me."

"Mmm—"

"When you wrote that last letter saying there was little time left in this sequence, what did you mean?"

Mother looked at me with perfect blankness.

I prompted, "You said, don't worry about time, I'll be there."

"Yes," she put down her cup. "Well, here I am!"

"But what did you *mean*?"

She had difficulty with my question. "Well, Jane, I *meant* for you not to worry about when I'd arrive. There was no reason to plan a time, meet me at the airport. Is that what you're asking?"

"And—no time left in the sequence?" I asked.

"Well! They have different groups coming at different times—there's a certain sequence. Jane! Did you think I *wasn't* coming back?"

I didn't want to answer that!

Something in her eyes said, well, you should have known better, but maybe it's not a bad thing that you did think that. On the other hand, who knows that it *wasn't* a possibility?

I asked her one other thing. "Mother, when you were there, working and everything, what was the time like? I mean, was it ever sort of—now?"

She got misty at that. "Sometimes . . . yes, sometimes it was like that. Like now."

Well, she wasn't going to say any more. And I didn't blame her. But I'd seen her first, you see—not daddy. And I figured that was going to be bad for him. He'd ask her questions she wasn't going to answer. I was right!

She had this serenity for the first few days she was home. She even moved differently. There was a split-second pause before she did anything. I was fascinated. In some dim way I could almost sense what she was doing.

Then it was equally fascinating to see it go. To watch her return, little by little, to a Western way of moving, as she got back into all the hurrying pace. But even that was a little different than before she'd left. She hurried, all right, but she didn't seem quite so agonized that it might not be done—all the work, I mean.

But my mother had really become fascinating to me. Like an object that's been around for years and you never noticed, but suddenly you do, and there's a mystery about it. Sometimes I'd catch glimpses of us all as fishes in that little pond. We were alike in all respects, but mother swam just a little bit differently from the rest of us, making smaller bubbles.

It really piqued Dick and daddy's curiosity. I could

feel sparks in the air. They sort of resented that she wasn't providing them with a travelogue. Of course if she *had* gone to Miami, they wouldn't have had any questions at all!

And mother didn't say a word. The thing that most irritated my father was her total absence of guilt. She never apologized, never offered any "explanation," never excused herself. She acted calmly, as if she expected him to "understand."

Understand the reasonableness of someone—even a *mother*—doing what they wanted and needed to do, once in a lifetime. Like a person in her own right and responsible to herself. It took a long time for them to reach even a truce about this. And even then it wasn't ever the same.

Mother had brought us all something from India. Again, it was interesting that she didn't give us these things right away. She waited a few days until she had settled in and we were all sort of used to each other. A lovely sari for me, a carved wooden elephant for Dick, and a hand-tooled Indian wallet for daddy. For herself she didn't have anything except a notebook of recipes. I expected the house to start smelling of curry right away but it didn't. Instead she cooked hamburgers for us and made pâté for daddy sometimes. It was weeks later, when I asked if she'd cook us an Indian dinner, that she got out her notebook.

Then I could see why she hadn't done this immediately. When my father came home and smelled that aroma he really tightened up. And after dinner it all came out, her going off to India, the terrible American Express bill, everything. They had a gorgeous fight!

I listened to it all from my room, with my ear pressed against the door, and I was thrilled! They fought beautifully! Before, you see, when they'd been

MLU's they *never* fought when we could hear them. At least, not anything you could really call *fighting*.

I don't mean to say that they didn't become MLU's again—in some little way. They did. I guess it's hard to get out of old habits. After the fight daddy quit his new job, mother went back to her old one, Dick went back to finish prep school, and they both treated me very nicely!

And I was able to go back to my good old comfortable private school. And in the position of being able to do almost anything I wanted. Except I couldn't! Every time I looked at mother and daddy I was reminded of the albums. I'd blink, and suddenly see them as five, or seventeen, or eighty years old. It was horrible! I knew what the conductor had been saying! I couldn't lie any more! They'd ask me something stupid, and I'd start to come up with a flip, put-down answer—and I couldn't do it! I'd hear music— "Lambeth Walk," "Happy Days Are Here Again," and in back of that I'd see *their* parents, my grandparents, and remember when my own mother and father weren't even born.

It was really almost funny. Silly. They'd look at me, expecting the absolute *worst* from me, this young generation—and I'd find myself hearing all these other echoes from *their* time, and doing what *they* asked me to do.

They couldn't understand it, and neither could I— except that I did. Mother may have "understood" a little. Sometimes I'd catch her looking at me with amusement. I just tried to remember what my conductor had said—go ahead and suffer, it's worth it in the end. I just plain suffered! I didn't find any "worth" in it at all until one day when I was outside, and there was Road Runner banking around our tree.

Well. I want you to know that I have *never* spoken to a five- or six-year-old child in my life! But I had recently been speaking to my over-forty-year-old parents, so I figured, what's the difference? And I said to Road Runner, feeling quite peculiar, "Hi."

He stopped instantly! And said, "Hiiiiiiiiiiiiiii!" Looking up at me with these astonished, beautiful eyes.

We both knew what it was all about. We went to the corner and had a cream soda together. And I looked at him and remembered Santa Claus. And knew he'd been right! Just for future reference, I taught Road Runner a song he hadn't known before. Guess which song! I'll give you a clue—Road Runner sang it to *his* mother at bedtime and freaked her out!

Here's something else that happened, which is totally unbelievable, except knowing my parents already and "understanding" that in their rock-bottom hearts they are truly MLU's, makes it not so unbelievable. Along with being an MLU, apparently, does go an ability to change, to drift with the new times, to have a sense of humor.

My mother and father, after going through this great big deal about gourmet lunches and drop-out to India bit—took their respective American Express cards, *framed* them in little individual glass cases, and hung them on their bedroom wall with a *hammer* between! You know those little "in case of fire" hammers? That was the general idea. They even put up a sign—BREAK IN CASE OF EMERGENCY!

Ah! Scorpio? I didn't see him again. I haven't found him yet. I kept going out, for many days after mother came home, but Harry always told me he hadn't been in. A month later I went out again, but still no one had seen him. That's when I knew that for me there'd be no more trains to Tottenville.

He has my name, though. Our telephone is listed under my father's name, and how could he ever forget Overbrook? I know he'll never forget Wanda. And even me, plain old Jane? He couldn't forget!

No, I won't go out again until the phone rings, or, in some other way, I know he's calling. I'm still terribly in love with Scorpio, and I don't know where he is or what he's doing. But someday I'm going to meet him again. And I hope then we won't have to be strangers.

I hear there are plans to change the Tottenville train into some fast super-charger. I don't care! I'll bet you anything my conductor will still be on that train. And I'll bet Scorpio will be there, too, in Tottenville. Ready to meet me, at the end, or the beginning of the line.

I'll Get There.
It Better Be
Worth The Trip.

by JOHN DONOVAN

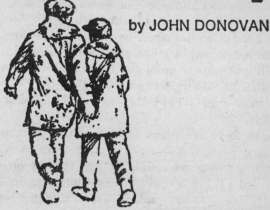

One of the most celebrated and discussed teenage novels of recent years, this is the perceptive and disarming story of a boy faltering on the brink of manhood. Torn between his loyalties to his divorced parents, whose own problems prevent them from understanding his loneliness, Davy shares his troubles with his only friend—his dachshund, Fred.

Then, at school, he meets Douglas, a boy from another broken home. Their mutual need for love and companionship propels them into a moment of open sexuality, and the painful aftermath drives Davy from childhood toward the new world of maturity.

A "Best Book of the Year"—*Library Journal*

Laurel-Leaf Library   75¢

Two Dogtown novels by Frank Bonham

THE NITTY GRITTY

If you live in a poor, black slum, you've got to hustle to live, but you've got to have a smart hustle to get out. Charlie Matthews wants to get out of Dogtown but the question is, How? The English teacher says stay in school. His father says shine shoes. When scheming Uncle Baron comes to town with get-rich-quick ideas, Charlie sees a light. He starts raising money to get in on the big deal and becomes a little wiser in the process.

"Real and tough!" —Chicago Tribune

❧❦❧

VIVA CHICANO

"I tried to be straight as an arrow, didn't I? But, man, it's not possible."

Keeny got started on a police record when he was a kid. Things never got much better. His father had taught him pride in *la raza*, but who could think about pride and being a Mexican when most of your life was filled with drugs, gangs, street fights, juvenile courts, and detention homes? When trouble started, people pointed to Keeny. So when he was accused of the murder of his little brother, Keeny ran. But he had to come back for one more fight against a world that didn't understand him.

"Taut and exciting . . . blistering candor."
—Saturday Review

LAUREL-LEAF BOOKS 75c each